WHAT DO YOU WANT
ON YOUR
PANCAKES?

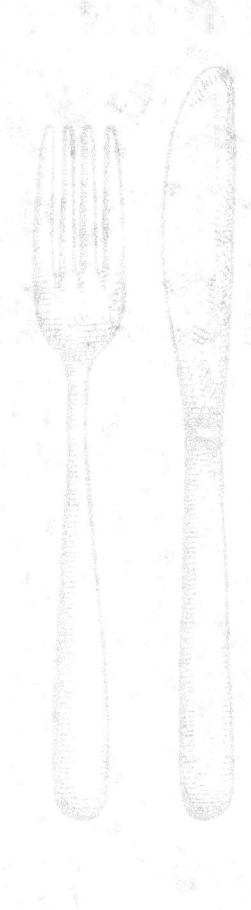

WHAT DO YOU WANT
ON YOUR
PANCAKES?

SHORT STORIES FOR ALL

Tom Fish | Gail Ritter
Anke Gross-Kunkel | Desi Doolin

proving
press

Book Design & Production:
Columbus Publishing Lab
www.ColumbusPublishingLab.com

Copyright © 2024 by
Chapters Ahead
LCCN: 2024926031

Paperback ISBN: 978-1-63337-866-7
E-Book ISBN: 978-1-63337-867-4

Printed in the United States of America
1 3 5 7 9 10 8 6 4 2

Table of Contents

"We dedicate our book to Mr. Robert Woodward and the GLOW Foundation. Their support and encouragement have made this work possible. We cannot thank them nearly enough."

Acknowledgments

DR. ANKE GROSS-KUNKEL would like to thank her husband for sharing life with her. She is grateful to her three children for keeping every day lively and giving her lots of ideas for new stories.

GAIL RITTER would like to recognize her husband, her family, her friends, her teachers, and her students for their encouragement and inspiration. "It takes a village!"

DESIREA DOOLIN would like to thank Day Program Learning Never Ends for their assistance and time helping with this book of short stories. She would also like to thank her family and friends for their unwavering support throughout life.

DR. TOM FISH appreciates the invaluable conviction, creativity, and support of his writing partners. This book was a team effort from start to finish. Also, kudos to Emily Hitchcock and Doug Davis at Proving Press for their goodwill, encouragement, and craftsmanship. Lastly, a big thanks to those with disabilities who have enriched the authors' lives in countless ways.

Foreword

FOR FAR TOO LONG, there has been a shortage of literature that addresses adult issues and experiences in a way that is both easily readable and meaningful for readers of all levels. That's what inspired us to write *What Do You Want on Your Pancakes?* Our collection of short stories and a play uses easy language, big print, and pictures to enhance readability and comprehension. We also make sure each page ends with a complete sentence.

Originally, we had the members of our Next Chapter Book Club (NCBC) in mind when writing *What Do You Want on Your Pancakes?* The Next Chapter Book Club is a literacy program established in 2002 at the Ohio State University by Dr. Tom Fish. NCBC is a community-based book club program for people with intellectual and developmental disabilities (IDD) that provides weekly opportunities for members to read and learn together, talk about books, and make friends in a community setting.

Beyond being full of easy-to-read selections, *What Do You Want on Your Pancakes?* is also interactive! The stories and the play include questions or thoughts interspersed throughout for the reader to consider. This was done to spark conversation and to help readers focus on the issues addressed in each selection.

Foreword

Another unique feature of this book is that, at the end of each selection, readers can access hands-on activities related to what they have just read. These activities are fun, creative, and can be completed either individually or as a group.

Having completed *What Do You Want on Your Pancakes?*, we realize that our targeted readership goes well beyond the members of our Next Chapter Book Clubs. We are hoping the selections in our book ring true with a wide range of readers. After all, everyone should have access to a good book! Happy reading, one and all!

What to Have on My Pancakes?

IT WAS SATURDAY MORNING. My week at work had felt like more than a month. All I was thinking about was going out for breakfast. After breakfast, I just wanted to come home and chill for the rest of the day. Having pancakes had been on my mind the last three days. Maybe I would call my brother, Adam, to see if he wanted to join me, but I was not sure yet.

What Do You Want on Your Pancakes?

My phone rang. I did not want to answer. If it was important, they would leave a message or call back. Unfortunately, I knew who was calling. I started thinking about what toppings I would have on my pancakes. The phone rang again. Darn it! I was right. It was Rob calling from work. I checked, and of course he had left a voicemail after the first call. "Hi Clair, it is Rob from work. I feel bad about calling on your day off. But we are having a big-time problem with the computer system here at work. Pretty please, can you call me? Maybe you can help me solve the problem over the phone. I really hope you get this message," he said. After swearing a few times to myself, I decided to call Rob back.

Trying to solve the computer system problem over the phone did not work. I was 90 percent sure it would not. But I tried. So much for pancakes this morning and chilling later in the day. After finding some clean clothes to wear, I arranged for an Uber, because I do not drive.

What to Have on My Pancakes?

Neither the driver nor I was interested in talking. I texted Rob to get a better idea about what the computer problem was. Rob texted back, but he did not have the information I needed. All it did was help kill time during the car ride.

Everyone was waiting for me. Rob had sent someone to get donuts for everyone. "The donuts look great. But pancakes were more on my mind this morning. Thanks, and now let's get to work," I said. It only took about an hour to solve the problem. As I was getting ready to leave, one of the staff members, Nancy Lane, asked if she could talk to me. I suggested we go to my office. As soon as I closed the door, Nancy began to cry.

"What is wrong, Nancy?" I asked.

She kept crying. I waited until she was done. I do not like it when people hand me a Kleenex when I am crying. It is like they are telling me to stop.

"Take all the time you need, Nancy. I am here to listen, whenever you are ready," I said.

Nancy was now starting to whimper. "I feel so embarrassed. The last thing I want to do is burden you with my problems. It is just that everything in my life is falling apart all at once," she said. It turns out Nancy had just broken up with her boyfriend, did not have enough money for a car payment, and was not getting along with her supervisor, Rob.

"Oh my, that is a lot to deal with all at once. How can I help?" I asked.

We spent the next half hour just talking, and I mostly listened.

QUESTIONS/THOUGHTS

- Do you like pancakes?
- What is your favorite food for breakfast?
- Do you ever feel like just chilling out?
- How do you feel when your plans have to change?

We did not solve Nancy's problems. She wasn't expecting me to wave a magic wand and fix everything. What we did do is start talking about some next steps she could take. I offered the name of a counselor who had helped me deal with some of my problems. I also invited her to join me for breakfast next Saturday and thought she might enjoy meeting my brother Adam.

Nancy could not stop thanking me. "Being able to let out some of my emotions today helped more than you know, Clair. I cannot thank you enough. Breakfast next Saturday is on me," she insisted.

What Do You Want on Your Pancakes?

On the Uber ride home, I thought more about how I could help Nancy. I wondered why she broke up with her boyfriend. What did she mean about not being able to get along with her supervisor, Rob? How would she get enough money to make her next car payment? I had no answer to these questions. Then a red light went off in my head. First, I do not know Nancy that well. Second, she has a lot of problems going on at the same time. Third, there is only so much I can do. Then it hit me. Rather than trying to solve Nancy's problems for her, I decided I should just be supportive.

When I got home, there was a note on my front door. It was from my next-door neighbor, Flip. He asked if I could come by to see him sometime over the weekend. I thought, *What could he want*?

Flip had been my neighbor for at least six years. We talked from time to time, but not a lot. He worked as a private investigator after retiring from the state police department.

What to Have on My Pancakes?

Since he lost his wife, Greta, three years ago, he had stopped working altogether. Flip, whose real name is Francis, had never left me a note before. I could not think of what he might want. My day was already turned upside down. Curious, I walked next door to talk with Flip.

Flip thanked me for coming over. Then he started to cry and get angry at the same time. "I can't take it anymore!" he yelled.

"What is going on, Flip?" I asked.

"I am having trouble with my next-door neighbors, Bob and Alice, and I miss my wife, Greta, like crazy. I also have no friends anymore. How is that for starters?" he said.

We sat down in the living room and Flip was still crying. I listened as he shared about how upset he had been. Turns out, Bob and Alice have wild parties in their backyard, and their trash ends up blowing into Flip's yard.

When he spoke to them, they said it was not their trash and that he was making a big deal out of nothing. "We are not speaking to each other. They just send me dirty looks, which I return," he said.

After spending a few hours with Flip, I was exhausted. It was midafternoon, and I was ready for a nap. I found myself thinking about what I could do to help Flip. Just like with Nancy, I wanted to figure out ways to solve Flip's problems for him. Then I remembered my decision from earlier when I spoke with Nancy: I can listen and support, but I can't solve everyone's problems. Before I fell off to sleep, I remembered a wise tale my mother used to share with me:

"I can't find my way out of this hole," said Tiny Dragon.

Big Panda smiled. "Then I will come and sit in it with you."

What to Have on My Pancakes?

It was 7:00 in the evening when I woke up. I had a lot going on today. Guess it tired me out. I started to think about my family. My younger brother, Adam, and I were adopted when he was three and I was six. Both of our parents died in a car crash while coming home from a movie. We had no relatives able or willing to raise us. Our adopted parents, Jody and Lester Stern, turned out to be the best parents ever. They never were able to have children. Mom (Jody) is a nurse, and Dad (Lester) owns a Nissan car dealership. Mom works part time at an urgent care center, and Dad is getting ready to sell his business in the next few years.

Our family is very close. Both Adam and I have disabilities. I have trouble seeing, and Adam has trouble learning. Mom and I talk every day. She is a rock for Adam and me. As much as Mom is a rock for us, Dad is a hammer. He never backs down when it comes to getting the support and services Adam and I need.

Mom and Dad have always said, "Be yourself, try hard, help others, and stand up for your rights." They expect a lot from us.

QUESTIONS/THOUGHTS

- How do you deal with more than one problem at the same time?
- Do you know anyone who has been adopted?
- What do you think about the advice Clair's mother and father gave her?

Adam and I have not had it easy. We both were bullied a lot at school. I wore thick glasses and people made fun of me. I did not just sit back and take the name-calling. I would say things like, "How would you like to be legally blind?" and "Do you know how bad I feel when you say mean things?" Adam put up with worse name-calling and people making fun of him than I did. When I was around, I stood up for him.

What to Have on My Pancakes?

No one was going to do or say mean things to my brother. Because of his intellectual disability, he was not so able to stick up for himself. However, now that he is a young adult, Adam is pretty good at dealing with people who are mean or who try to take advantage of him. Unfortunately, he has had a lot of practice.

Feeling fresh and hungry after my nap, I knew I needed to find something to eat. It was tough to think about what to eat now when I couldn't stop thinking about pancakes next Saturday! I decided I wanted something quick. I opened my freezer and pulled out a Red Baron pepperoni pizza. My mind was still thinking about pancakes next Saturday. Pizza in the next twenty minutes would be great, but there's nothing like a tall stack of pancakes, and who knows how many tasty toppings I will order. Yummy!

What Do You Want on Your Pancakes?

Just then, I got a text from my boyfriend, Wally. He was visiting his former roommate from college. *I am beat, but can we talk tomorrow morning?* his message said. That was fine with me, I had already had too many conversations on my day off! He ended his text with, *Miss you, Clair, and by the way, how were the pancakes you were looking forward to this morning?*

If only Wally knew what I had been through today. I would share all the details tomorrow when he called. The computer system glitch, the crying, the decisions, all of it. At least the Red Baron pepperoni pizza was fantastic, and so were the two love stories I picked out to watch on my TV that night while wearing my comfiest pajamas. It was a fun ending to a day filled with ups and downs.

The phone rang. It was Sunday morning, and I had been sound asleep. It was Wally calling. I tried to be upbeat when I answered the phone. "Hi, sweetie!" I said, trying to sound happy and awake.

Wally was in a good mood because he had just been out for breakfast with his former roommate Gabe. "Guess what I had for breakfast? Since I was missing you, I decided to order pancakes, even though I was in the mood for bacon and eggs. The pancakes were okay. The problem was they were out of whipped cream and a lot of toppings I wanted, like bananas and chopped nuts. They had syrup, but it tasted kind of watery. Anyway, enough about me, how were your pancakes yesterday?" he asked.

13

I gave him the short version of how my day had gone. Wally was very kind and understanding. Then he told me about the good news.

It turns out Wally had been offered the possibility of a job. That is right: a job as an air-traffic controller in Phoenix.

"But we live in Kansas City," I blurted out.

"I know. This came as a surprise. Gabe's brother-in-law is an air-traffic controller, and he told me that there are a couple of job openings. I even talked to the head supervisor. It would not be a sure thing, but they have openings. And of course, Phoenix is a cool town with so many outdoor things to do. Just think, there would be no more snow and cold weather to deal with. What do you think, Clair?"

I told him that was an unfair question to ask without giving me some time to think about it. "Can we talk more about it when you get home?" I asked.

What to Have on My Pancakes?

By the time Wally came home, he had changed his mind about moving to Phoenix. He did not tell me exactly why. I think it may have had something to do with my reaction. But he said there were several factors that entered his decision. I was very happy. Wally knows how close I am to my family. We did not talk too much because Wally had just come back from his trip. Mostly, we hugged.

The new week got off to a flying start. I really did not have much time to think about all that had gone on over the weekend. My phone rang. Guess who it was? If you guessed Rob from the office, you were right. "You are not going to believe this, Clair. Our office in Denver needs you there by this afternoon. I know it is short notice, but can you be ready in an hour? I have asked Nancy to go with you to help you get around and support you with the problem they are having in Denver. If you never want to talk to me again, I will understand," he said.

"You are right, Rob; I do not want to speak with you again, or at least not for a few weeks."

"Can you be ready to go in an hour?" Rob questioned.

"Yes, I can be ready in an hour. How long is this trip going to take?" I asked.

Rob said Nancy and I would only be gone for one or two nights. He was sending a car to take us to the airport, and we had first-class airline tickets. I thought I was going to go back to my normal routine after this weekend with twists and turns. I guess not! I will do my best to go with the flow. When I took this job I knew there would be times when I had to do things or go places without much notice.

QUESTIONS/THOUGHTS

- Have you ever stood up for a friend or relative who was being made fun of?
- If you were Clair, would you have been upset with Rob?

- How do you deal with last minute changes?
- Have you ever been on an airplane, and if so, how did you like it?

I enjoyed the plane trip with Nancy. She helped me get around in the airport because of my vision problems. She had already reached out to a counselor, someone who was going to help her deal with the problems she had shared with me on Saturday. We enjoyed one another's company. It turned out that Nancy had a cousin by the name of Penny. Penny also had an intellectual disability and was two years younger than my brother, Adam. "Small world," I said.

After a few minutes of talking about our families and places we liked to shop, the topic changed to food. It turned out that Nancy was as wild about pancakes as I was. Before we knew it, the plane was getting ready to land in Denver.

"Listen, Nancy, I have a great idea. Maybe we can talk about it tonight if that is okay with you?" I asked.

Nancy said she was eager to find out what I was thinking.

Nancy and I worked until 7:00 and then had dinner at a diner close to our hotel. The people at work wanted to take us out, but we agreed to go the next night.

"So, what is the great idea you talked about on the plane?" Nancy asked.

"I think we should plan a pancake party and invite some friends and family. Do you think we could pull it off by this Saturday morning?" I asked.

"It only gives us a few days, but why not try?" Nancy said with a great big smile on her face.

We spent the next few hours talking about the party. We also agreed to start work early the next morning so that we could fly back home tomorrow night instead of Wednesday. We were like two teenagers planning for a slumber party.

What to Have on My Pancakes?

The next few days were a great deal of fun. We sent out virtual invitations for our party that read:

JOIN US THIS SATURDAY
Throw all your cares away
Pancakes we will eat
Maybe some other treats
Fun we will have
Come happy not sad

Happy trails until then!!
RSVP to Clair or Nancy

By the way, we are meeting at
Herman's Breakfast Place at 10:00
in the private dining room

A secret friend is paying
so leave your money at home

What Do You Want on Your Pancakes?

Nancy and I decided to invite Rob, and we also asked him to pay for breakfast. He said he would pay because he had not been very nice lately. Rob was going to be away on Saturday, but he thanked us for inviting him. Everyone else said they would be there. I invited my brother, Adam, my boyfriend, Wally, my neighbor Flip, my girlfriend Wanda, and my mother, Jody. My dad works on Saturday mornings, or I would have invited him. Nancy invited her cousin Penny, her boyfriend (even though they had broken up), two girlfriends from her workout class, and her father. Nancy and I were excited to meet each other's friends and family. Once we knew for sure who was coming, we made a reservation and sent out a list of pancake toppings that would be available at Herman's Breakfast Place.

The rest of the week went on as normal, and I was very thankful for that. I woke up in the best mood on Saturday. I got to Herman's ten minutes early, because I was so excited to eat with friends and family.

What to Have on My Pancakes?

Nancy and I chose Herman's because they have the best menu for pancakes. Each patron would be allowed four toppings per pancake order. You could choose from the following: whipped cream, marshmallows, cherries, strawberries, pineapple, bananas, blueberries, chocolate, caramel, maple syrup, mixed nuts, colored sprinkles, chocolate morsels, and crushed Heath bars. There were so many choices, it made me realize how overwhelmed I was after all of the choices I had to make over the last week. I made my final choice of the morning by going with my usual order: pancakes with whipped cream and strawberries!

Breakfast was a big hit. Everyone enjoyed their pancakes, except my mom, who ordered oatmeal. She is one of the few people I know who is not crazy about pancakes. I had a blast. A lot had gone on over the week. Lots of ups and downs. But friendships and pancakes were priceless. I told everyone that I was going to go home and chill out for the rest of the day.

FOR FUN ACTIVITIES RELATED TO OUR STORIES,
USE THE QR CODE PROVIDED.

Agree to Disagree

MY NAME IS CHARLES, but my family calls me Chick. Maybe it has something to do with the fact that I live on a farm in Central Iowa that has lots of chickens. By the way, Iowa produces more corn, eggs, and pork than any other state in the US. Getting back to the name Chick, it is mostly my family that calls me that. My friends call me Charlie.

Our farm is about four hundred acres. We grow corn and soybeans. I live with my mother and father and older brother, Phil. My mother raises chickens and goats. We have two family horses called Happy and Lucky.

What Do You Want on Your Pancakes?

My brother Phil and I take care of the horses and about twenty-five pigs. But I won't bore you with all their names. Mom and Dad are teachers at the local high school. Before and after work, Mom and Dad tend to their chores around the farm. To say we are a busy family would be an understatement. Chores are a BIG part of life for us. Tending to the animals and crops, repairing broken farm equipment, and making sure that things are neat and tidy around the house and in the barn are very important. With Mom and Dad both being teachers, it is important to get our chores done on time.

I like some chores more than others. Feeding Happy and Lucky is cool because they always seem glad to see me. Maybe that has something to do with the fact that I usually have a few carrots and apples in my pocket. The pigs, on the other hand, can be a royal pain sometimes. They tend to smell and can get nasty too. My brother Phil helps a little with the horses and pigs but mostly tends to the soybeans and corn with our dad. Phil is older than me by five years and works full time on the farm.

QUESTIONS/THOUGHTS

- Do you have chores that you are responsible for? If so, what are they?
- Would you like to live on a farm? Why or why not?
- What farm animal would you like to be for a day?

What Do You Want on Your Pancakes?

I just graduated from high school and have a part-time job at Ricky's Drive-In where I mostly do prep work in the kitchen. That means I help the cooks by preparing food. I also wash dishes and clean up around the kitchen. I was trained in high school for food service. I do not have my driver's license yet, so my family must drive me to and from work. The main reason I do not drive is because I have autism. Driving makes me very nervous, and I am not good at making quick decisions. Maybe someday I will be more comfortable behind the wheel, who knows? For now, I must depend on my family to drive me places.

Phil is my driver most of the time. He is usually okay with it. But there are times he wishes I would hurry up and get my driver's license.

I like to think of myself as a responsible person. I work hard and usually get things done on time. However, there is one exception. I hate to make my bed! Mom and Dad have tried to explain the importance of making the bed.

They list the following reasons:

- You will feel better.
- Doing so is the sign of a neat person.
- It only takes a few minutes.
- It starts your day off right.
- It encourages you to keep your bedroom neat and tidy.
- It helps you become more productive.
- It lowers stress and improves your mood.
- It just looks and feels better and makes the bedroom look cleaner.

My response to them is:

- It seems like a waste of time.
- No one is going to see it anyway.
- I have more important things to do.
- It is just going to get messed up again anyway.
- It is my bed, and I should be the one to decide if it gets made or not.

What Do You Want on Your Pancakes?

Like I said, my mom and dad would like me to make my bed more often. Mom recently gave me a pep talk, saying, "Listen, Chick, a neat bed is important. At some point you might want to move out on your own. I worry you will not take care of your place. I know you can do it. Could you just please try a little harder?"

I responded by saying, "I hear you, Mom. Let me see what I can do about it." I did not want to have an argument with my mother. When I get into arguments with other people it makes me feel very nervous and angry. But at the same time, I really did not want to make my bed.

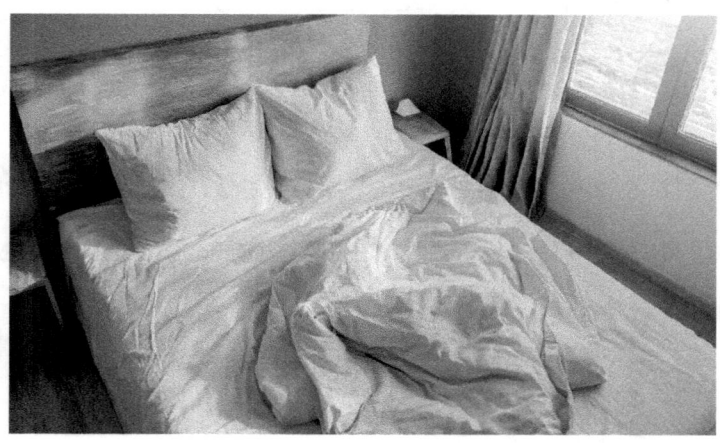

QUESTIONS/THOUGHTS

- What do you think about making your bed every day?
- Have you ever gotten into an argument with your mom or dad? How did it make you feel?

The next day I was scheduled to work at Ricky's Drive-In. I was excited to get away from the farm, mostly because of the lecture my mom had given me about my bed. On the ride from the farm, Phil got on my case about making my bed too. He agreed with my mom and dad. He started by saying, "Hey, Chick, you are a great guy, and I love having you as my brother. I only want what is best for you. I know Mom and Dad have been talking to you about the importance of making your bed. I have to say I agree with them. Making a bed is like brushing your teeth and combing your hair. I also think if you made your bed every morning it would be a great way to get your day off to a good start.

"Okay, I am done. I only want what is best for you, Chick, and to help you become as independent as you can be."

I told Phil that I would try to do better. But I really was thinking that he should mind his own business. I didn't tell him how to run his life. I should be able to do anything I wanted to do in my own bedroom.

Everyone at Ricky's was glad to see me. They all knew about my autism and some of the special challenges that came along with it. I learned in high school about the importance of speaking up for myself. For me this meant being open to others about my needs. For example, I can become nervous when I am not sure what people are asking me. Sometimes I also go on and on about certain things, like the history of horses, even when other people are not interested. Loud noises and being close to people are hard for me. It also takes me longer than most people to understand what people are saying to me.

Sometimes they need to explain it to me in a couple of different ways until I get it. Anyway, I was happy to be at work after the hard time my family had given me about not making my bed.

Ricky is the owner and head chef at the drive-in. He is a hard worker and wants the people that work for him to do the same. However, Ricky likes to have fun and is very easy to talk to. He always seems to know what is going on at the drive-in. Ricky saw me as I was walking in to start work. "Hey, what's up, Charlie?" he asked.

I did not want to tell him about all I had been through with my family, so I said, "I am fine."

Ricky knew from the sound of my voice that something was not right. "It does not sound like things are fine. I am always here if you want to talk about what is on your mind," Ricky said.

I walked past Ricky and replied, "No, you are right. Things are not great. Maybe we could talk about it when you have some time. Right now, I probably should get to work. Thanks, Ricky, for being so concerned."

I got busy washing tomatoes, potatoes, and lettuce. Then I asked Alfredo, one of Ricky's chefs, what he wanted me to do next. Alfredo is my direct supervisor. He is like a second brother to me.

"You don't seem like yourself today, Charlie. Is something on your mind?" Alfredo asked.

"Ricky told me the same thing. My parents and brother have been after me to make my bed. I feel like telling them to mind their own business. I know they are just trying to teach me good habits. However, I am an adult now, and except at work, I don't like being told what to do."

Alfredo did not say anything right away. After a long pause he took a deep breath and said, "I understand how you feel, Charlie. I can see two things going on. The first is, you don't like making your bed, and the second is, you don't like being told what to do."

"You got that right, Alfredo," I replied.

Alfredo took another deep breath and said, "The only thing is, Charlie, there are some things in life we do because they will make us feel better. I read a report that said people who make their beds feel happier and like they get a lot of things done. For me, making my bed is the first task of my day.

What Do You Want on Your Pancakes?

"It is something that only takes two minutes, the report says. Sure, I skip a day here and there, but not often. I think if you begin to make your bed you may come to see that it is easier than it seems. Ok, I will shut up now. But just one more thing. Remember, Charlie, your family cares about you."

I said, "Thanks for the pep talk, Alfredo. You have given me a lot to think about. I probably should be getting back to work. I will keep you posted."

After my talk with Alfredo, I washed some dishes and cleaned the kitchen floor. It felt good to finish my tasks. I was proud of the job I had done.

Just then Ricky came by. "Everything looks good in here, Charlie. Keep up the great work. Are you feeling better now than when you first came in today?" he asked.

"I sure am. Alfredo and I had a talk. He gave me a lot to think about. But I am still sorting things out," I said.

"Take your time, Charlie. There is no need to rush when you are trying to decide about something. I once bought a purple coat that was on sale and could not be returned. When I got it home, my brother Paul told me it looked like something he saw a clown wear at the circus. After thinking about it, I agreed with him. At first, I was upset with myself for buying something I would never wear. Then I realized, not all decisions are going to be perfect in life.

"The thing is, you will not know if a decision is okay or not until you have made it. Good luck, Charlie. See you later," Ricky said.

A lot of thoughts were going through my head as I waited for my brother Phil to pick me up after work. He usually was on time but not today. I started to think that maybe something was wrong. I do have a cell phone, but it has not been working lately. Phil keeps saying he will take me to the phone store to get it fixed. I thought about going back into work and asking to borrow a phone but did not want to bother anybody. Then I started to worry even more about why Phil was late. When I worry my feet start to shake and I pull on my hair. Just then I heard honking and saw Phil's beat-up old Ford pickup truck heading toward me. I don't think I have ever been happier to see someone.

"Sorry for being late, Chick. I bet you were getting upset with me. I am also sorry that we have not gone to get your phone fixed. Truth is, I was busy taking care of a sick pig. You would not have been able to reach me even if your phone was working. I hope you will accept my apology," Phil said.

I told Phil that, yes, I was upset with him. I also said I was worried that something bad had happened. He told me he loved me, and I told him I would not trade him for any other brother in the world.

"Even though I have been getting on you about making your bed?" he asked.

"Yes," I said. "The bed thing has gotten out of hand. I wish we all could just agree to disagree for a while. Maybe we could take a time-out like they do in football, only for longer."

I saw Phil nod his head up and down. He seemed happy to not talk about the bed for a while. We did not talk the rest of the way home.

I was tired when we got home. I ran into the house and got a few carrots for Happy and Lucky. They were happy to see me and lucky to get a carrot treat. All I could think of next was going to my bedroom for a nap before dinner. I could not wait to jump on the bed and close my eyes. When I jumped on my bed, I heard a loud crack. It was not a good sound. A few seconds later my bed fell to the ground. *There goes my nap*, was my first thought. Then I got mad at myself for jumping on the bed. What should I do next? Maybe my dad could fix it?

The bed is old, so maybe I needed a new one. I was very confused about what to do next. With so many thoughts going on in my brain, I closed my eyes and tried to relax.

"Chick, it is time for dinner!" Phil yelled as he pounded on my door.

The nap felt great. But what should I say to my family? I started to worry, then suddenly I had an idea. My parents and Phil were waiting for me at the dinner table. Mom had made spaghetti, salad, and garlic bread—my favorites. Everyone was looking at me.

"Let's start eating," I said. Then I told them a joke: "Where do you take a bed to get it fixed after someone jumps on it and breaks it? To the nearest dump, that's where! Because bed doctors do not make house calls."

My family looked at me and did not know what to think. Then my dad, who was usually very serious, started to laugh. Before long we were all laughing. When the laughing stopped, I told them what had happened to my bed. I asked my mom if she would help me shop for a new bed.

She gave me a serious look and said, "Sure, honey, but only if you promise to make it every day." Then my mom started laughing and said, "See, Chick, you are not the only one in this family who can tell a joke."

We finally started to eat dinner. We made some more jokes and laughed together. I agreed to make my new bed more often. My parents and brother agreed not to get on my case so much when I didn't make my bed.

I think we were finally able to agree to disagree. I did not want to tell them, but I was pretty sure my new bed would be looking pretty every day. I was feeling good about it!

QUESTIONS/THOUGHTS

- When was the last time you told or heard a joke? Do you remember what it was?
- Charlie says that his family has agreed to disagree. What does that mean? Do you think it is a good thing to agree to disagree?
- Do you like to laugh? Do it now!

FOR FUN ACTIVITIES RELATED TO OUR STORIES,
USE THE QR CODE PROVIDED.

Finally On Vacation

"ALL ABOARD!" The conductor had a loud deep voice and sounded like I thought he would. I had never been on a train before and was very excited. A big smile came over my face. Mom had gone to check out the diner car. We were both looking forward to having lunch there. It would be very cool to have my first meal on my first train ride.

"All aboard!" I heard another conductor say, but this time it was a woman. "Everyone please be seated for departure," she said.

Seconds later, my mom took her seat next to me. Mom thought it was great that the train had a female conductor. As she began to tell me about the lunch menu, the train started to move, and I turned to Mom and said, "I am finally on vacation!"

Mom and I had a sleeper room with seats that folded out into beds at night. Since the trip from Spokane, Washington (our hometown), to Chicago, Illinois, would take forty-two hours, we wanted to get two good nights of sleep. Once the train left the station, we first passed places we knew, like our favorite dog park and the local Coke bottling plant.

It was not long before the train entered the state of Idaho. Shortly after that, the two conductors came by to check our tickets and see if we were comfortable. We found out their names were Harry and Hilda. They could not have been nicer.

"I see you are traveling to Chicago. What brings you there?" Harry asked.

"I have never been to Chicago or on a train before," I told him. What I did not tell Harry and Hilda was how hard it had been for me to decide where to go on vacation, who to go with, and how to pay for it. More about that later. Hilda and Harry said how happy they were that we were on board and to let them know if we needed anything.

Mom and I were getting hungry and left for the diner car. I was hoping pizza would be on the menu. Mom told me it was.

QUESTIONS/THOUGHTS

- Have you ever been on a train, and if so, what kind was it, and what was it like?
- When was your last vacation, and where did you go?

Before departing on vacation, I was hard at work at my Aunt Jenn's pet shop. The name of the shop is Bow Wow Meow. Aunt Jenn is a lot of fun. On Halloween every year she dresses up as a different animal. Once a month she opens the shop for customers to bring their pets in for a pet parade. I love working at Bow Wow Meow because my coworkers, boss, and customers all enjoy being there. My job at the shop is to stock shelves. I bring out pet food and stuff like that and make sure it is neatly arranged on the shelves. I am not very tall, nor do I weigh that much, but I am strong and do not mind working hard.

Just after lunch that day, Aunt Jenn asked if she could speak with me in private. I did not know what it was about. When we walked into her office, she asked me to close the door. Now I was starting to get worried. Turns out I did not need to be.

"You know, Paula, you are my favorite niece, and I want you to be happy," she said. Of course I am her favorite niece, because I am her only niece. She and my mom are sisters.

"I am happy, Aunt Jenn, and you are the best boss ever," I told her.

"Well, your best boss ever is giving you two weeks off. You have been working here for three years and have not taken any vacation time. We have talked about this before. You need to take time off! Go wherever you want and do whatever you like, but do not show up for work for two weeks. I will give you three weeks to make your plans, and then you are off." She ended. We talked a little longer and parted on good terms. I took a deep breath and started to think about planning my vacation.

Aunt Jenn was right. I had been dragging my feet about taking a vacation. Here are some of the reasons why:

- I did not want to go anywhere by myself. Who would go with me?
- I was not sure where to go.
- If I stayed home during my time off, it would not feel like a real vacation.
- I am a picky eater.

- I get very nervous in new places.
- Would I be able to take my helper dog, Skippy, wherever I went?
- Would I have enough money to pay for the trip?

With such a long list, I had never gotten very far planning a vacation. That is why I had not taken one in three years. Oh boy, what to do now? I only had three weeks to make my plans. For me, that felt like a very short time because I HAVE A LOT OF TROUBLE MAKING DECISIONS!

QUESTIONS/THOUGHTS

- What do you think of pet stores? Do you smile when you go in?
- Is deciding easy or hard for you?

What Do You Want on Your Pancakes?

I guess it's about time I tell you a little about myself. My name is Paula Fields. I am twenty-two years old and live with my mom. We share a three-bedroom house in Spokane, Washington. My dad died after a heart attack when I was thirteen. I miss him every day. Dad owned a local hardware store, and mom now owns and manages it. Every year mom and I ride in a forty-mile bicycle charity event to raise money for cancer research.

I know Dad would be proud of Mom and me. I am an only child. The only relatives we have close by are my Aunt Jenn and her husband, Ronnie, who is a professional comedian. He is really funny and calls me his little brussels sprout. Ronnie is gone a lot making people laugh all over the country, mostly at comedy clubs. Aunt Jenn and Ronnie were unable to have children. I am like a daughter to them, and that makes me happy.

Now I want to talk about Skippy. He is my dog. He helps calm me down when I get worried and nervous. He was trained for two years to be a helper dog. I do not know what I would do without Skippy. He protects me and gives me confidence. He is also the sweetest and cutest thing in the world.

What Do You Want on Your Pancakes?

I have two close girlfriends I have known since first grade. We hang out a lot together. Their names are Beth and Mindy. We call ourselves the first-graders. We all have boyfriends, but nothing too serious. My boyfriend is Sherman, and we work together at Bow Wow Meow. Sherman thinks we should get married, but I am not so sure. He understands me, but sometimes treats me like a little kid. I do not like that.

It was Saturday morning, and my head was spinning. Only two more weeks to decide what to do about vacation. I had been asking friends and family what they thought I should do. They gave me ideas but mostly asked what I wanted to do. Some of the ideas I had come up with so far were:

- Stay home and paint my bedroom. I could also volunteer to pick up trash along the highway.
- Take a cruise to Alaska.
- Drive to the redwoods in California.
- Go to Chicago to see the art museum and eat deep-dish pizza.

- Gamble and see shows in Las Vegas.
- Hike the Grand Canyon and go rafting on the Colorado River.

My Uncle Ronnie was in town on a break from his latest comedy tour. He asked me to join him for lunch. Even though my head was spinning, I was pretty sure Uncle Ronnie would cheer me up. We met at a place called the Twisted Rooster Bar and Grill. I left Skippy at home because I rode my bike. Ronnie was talking with Stella, the bar owner, when I arrived. Of course, he introduced me as his little brussels sprout. Stella said she knew Ronnie from back in high school. She told me, "Ronnie was the class clown and could even make the teachers laugh. Have whatever you want for lunch, Paula, because lunch is on me."

Once we were seated, Ronnie smiled and began to speak. "You mean the world to your aunt and me, Paula. Jenn tells me that she is making you take a vacation. We want to pay for your trip."

I could not believe what he just said! "Do you mean that, or is this some kind of joke?" I asked. I knew he was serious, but I just had to ask. Boy, how cool is that? He also said that he and Jenn had arranged for my mom to go with me. "I can't believe how kind and generous you and Aunt Jenn have been to me," I said with tears in my eyes. The next thing I knew, I was up out of my seat and giving Uncle Ronnie the biggest hug ever. I was excited, thankful, and happy, all at the same time. "This has to be one of the happiest days of my life!" I said while kissing Uncle Ronnie on both cheeks.

QUESTIONS/THOUGHTS
- Do you know any funny people?
- On a scale from 1 to 10, with 10 being the funniest, how funny are you?
- Have you ever lost a loved one, and if so, what was it like?

I felt like clicking my heels like Dorothy in *The Wizard of Oz*. The only problem was, I was riding my bike, so I couldn't do it. I wanted to tell the world, but I thought I would start with Beth, Mindy, and Sherman. Then it hit me. I was going on vacation with my mom in two weeks. But—there were so many decisions to be made. My happiness level dropped, and my worry level increased! I said out loud to myself, "You have a lot to do, young lady!"

QUESTIONS/THOUGHTS

- Have you ever felt great one minute and not so great the next?
- Have you ever had to make a decision quickly? If so, what did it feel like?

What Do You Want on Your Pancakes?

The first thing I did at home was make a to-do list of everything I had to decide before Mom and I went on our vacation. Here is my list:

- Where should we go?
- Would I be able to take Skippy?
- If not, where would he stay?
- Do I want to go for the whole two weeks?
- Can I find restaurants that have food I like?
- Do I need new clothes for the trip?
- What suitcase do I take?

After my to-do list, I wrote a poem to myself:

Very little time left
Take a great big breath
Try not to delay
Figure out a way
You just have to decide
Then go along for the ride
Good luck and get going!

Finally On Vacation

My friends Beth and Mindy were coming over that night to hang out with me. They are very supportive and always want what is best for me. We talked for a long time about my upcoming vacation, and they had lots of different ideas about where I should go and what I should do. But at the end of the evening, I was more confused than ever about what to do.

What Do You Want on Your Pancakes?

The following day, Sherman and I went roller-skating. We had a lot of fun. I wasn't sure if I wanted to ask him for his advice about my vacation, but I did. Sherman could not have been nicer. We sat outside the skating rink for a long time after we had finished skating, and he listened to me as I explained the trouble I was having making decisions about my upcoming vacation.

He had a great idea. "Sometimes it helps me to ask myself the questions: who, where, what, when, why, and how," he explained. My brain was already trying to answer the questions after he told me. I owed Sherman a big hug, and I decided to bring him a treat back from the trip.

Here is what I came up with:

- Who? I am going with my mom, and still need to see if Skippy can go.
- Where? I am leaning toward Chicago because of the famous art museum and deep-dish pizza that is supposed to be amazing. I could eat pizza every day.

- What? This is easy: It is vacation.
- Why? Because I need one and I have no choice.
- When? In less than two weeks.
- How? The first part of this is easy: Ronnie and Jenn are paying me to go wherever I decide to go, like Chicago. I need to decide how to get there and find out how much it will cost.

I felt a lot better after thinking about these questions. Then I remembered the poem I had written. It said to take a deep breath, not to delay, figure out a way, and you just have to decide. With that I took a great big breath. Then it came to me: I was going to Chicago. Knowing where I was going was a big weight off my shoulders. I still needed to figure out how to get there, where to stay and for how long, what the trip would cost, and whether Skippy would be able to go.

The next day I told my mom about my decision to visit Chicago. She was excited because she had never been there either. We agreed to go for ten days. That would give us time before the trip to get ready, and afterward to unwind before going back to work. Mom said, "I have an idea about how we may be able to travel to Chicago and see a lot of America at the same time. If we took a train, we might also be able to take Skippy."

Mom talked to her friend Hal, who is a lawyer. He said we would be allowed to take Skippy because he is my helper dog. The nice thing about the train between Spokane and Chicago is that it makes a lot of stops. My mom is the best. She had even thought about how the train stopping a lot would be good for Skippy to have bathroom breaks. I was finally getting comfortable about my vacation plans.

Only two more things left to do. I needed to figure out where we would stay in Chicago, and then, of course, how much the trip would cost. I started to worry again. But as it turns out, I did not need to. Mom had told Aunt Jenn about my decision to vacation in Chicago. When I got to work the next morning, Aunt Jenn called me into her office again.

She looked at me and said, "I know it has not been easy for you to decide where to go. Your mom tells me that you want to take a train and have Skippy go along with you. Ronnie and I will take care of making your travel and hotel arrangements. That way everything will be paid for before you leave."

Again, I felt like kicking my heels and was actually able to. *What a lucky young lady I am*, I thought to myself. Jenn could see how happy I was. We both shed tears of joy and made good use of the new tissue box on her desk.

QUESTIONS/THOUGHTS
- Who do you turn to for support?
- Are you a picky eater?
- Where do you want to go on your next vacation? It is never too early to start planning.

FOR FUN ACTIVITIES RELATED TO OUR STORIES,
USE THE QR CODE PROVIDED.

Vacation, Part 2

HI, IT IS PAULA AGAIN. I was the person in the last story deciding where to go on vacation. I finally decided to take the train to Chicago from my home in Spokane, Washington. Remember?

The last story began with my mom and me on the train getting ready to leave the station. We met the conductors, Hilda and Harry. They were nice and helpful. I could not have been happier. The story ended with my Aunt Jenn and me sharing tears of joy. In between the beginning and the end of the story, I was on an emotional roller coaster. That was then, and this is now.

Mom and I were in the diner car having dinner. My helper dog, Skippy, was in our sleeper car. Mom was right about my favorite food, pizza, being on the menu. I was thrilled. Mom could not decide what to order. "I'm trying to decide on the meatloaf or the sea bass," she said. She went for the meatloaf. Mom enjoyed it and had apple pie for dessert. It was so much fun eating dinner and being able to see the beautiful scenery outside. We were both full from dinner. By the way, I had a hot fudge sundae after my pizza. When we got back to the sleeper car, Skippy was happy to see us. The train was stopping, so I took Skippy out to do his business. When we got back, Mom was sleeping.

QUESTIONS/THOUGHTS
- Would you have chosen meatloaf or sea bass?
- Do you have a favorite dessert?
- What do you think it would be like to have dinner on a train?

Early the next morning, I heard Mom moaning. I was concerned and asked her what was wrong. She said she was in pain. "Could you please have Hilda or Harry come check on me?" she asked. I told her I would be right back and to try to stay calm. It did not take long to find Hilda. I told her my mother had become sick after dinner. Hilda followed me back to our sleeper car. Mom had fallen back to sleep. As we entered our car, my mom woke up. She told Hilda that she was having stomach pain, thought she may have a fever, and felt dizzy. Now I was worried.

Hilda told Mom that she would return soon. Hilda asked me to join her outside the sleeper car. We walked to a private area. "I am concerned about your mother, Paula. I am going to find Harry, and we will see if there is a doctor or nurse on the train. In the meantime, I want you to go back and stay with your mom and Skippy," she said. I was shaking but went back to our car and waited. Mom was still asleep. I began to think the worst. What if she needed to be in the hospital? Who would stay with me? Would she be able to make it all the way to Chicago? A million more questions were going through my mind.

Within a few minutes, a doctor had been found.

The doctor was a retired family doctor who was travelling to see her son in Chicago. Her name was Dr. Waters. She asked to be alone while she examined Mom. I stood outside with Hilda and Harry. They both did everything they could to calm me down. Harry even told a few jokes to get my mind off what was happening.

Just as I finished laughing at Harry's last joke ("What do you call a large angry cow? A big mad moo") Dr. Waters came out of our room. She had a serious look on her face. Mom had given her permission to talk with me and the train staff. "I think we need to get your mom to the nearest hospital. She is having serious abdominal pain. I want to make sure we find out what is causing her pain," she explained.

QUESTIONS/THOUGHTS

- Do you have a favorite joke or funny story?
- Do you think it is good to laugh, and if so, why?
- How many times a week do you laugh?
- Do you have a favorite doctor, and what do you like about them?

What Do You Want on Your Pancakes?

I felt like fainting after hearing from the doctor. Hilda and Harry could tell I was upset. They found a place for me to sit down. The doctor returned to Mom. I could not believe what was going on, and of course I was feeling worried. While Harry stayed with me, Hilda went off to make plans for getting Mom to the nearest hospital. Luckily, the train's next stop, in about fifteen minutes, was Minneapolis, Minnesota. Harry kept checking to see if I was okay, and he asked if there was anyone I wanted to call. Of course, I wanted to call Aunt Jenn to tell her what was going on. Harry let me use his phone because I had left mine behind in the sleeper car. I told him the phone number and asked him to explain the situation to my aunt. He did a great job of letting Aunt Jenn know what was going on and then handed the phone to me. Aunt Jenn wanted to take a few minutes to think about things and would call me back. I tried to take deep breaths to calm myself down. It seemed to help.

Aunt Jenn called back, and Harry answered his phone and told my aunt that I was being a real trooper. He then handed me the phone. Here is what she had to say. "I know you are worried, Paula. So am I. The main thing now is to wait and see what the doctors say. Soon you will go with your mom to the hospital by ambulance. The train staff has made arrangements for Skippy to stay at a very nice animal spa near the hospital. I have spoken to the spa owner, and she is looking forward to meeting Skippy. I have also planned for Sherman to fly to Minneapolis. Hopefully, he will provide help and support for you. I booked a hotel room for him two blocks from the hospital. He should arrive by noon tomorrow. You will stay overnight at the hospital with your mom. That is about it for now. Call me once you get to the hospital. I know this is a lot to take in. Any questions, Paula?"

I told Aunt Jenn I had a lot of questions, but they could wait. I felt like jumping through the phone to hug her. I was excited to see my boyfriend, Sherman, and thanked her for sending him to be with Mom and me. I began to think how lucky I was to have such a wonderful family.

The train began to slow down. Dr. Waters had Harry stay with Mom while she talked to me. She was calm but very serious. She told me my mom was doing okay. She had spoken several times with the emergency room doctor to update her on Mom's condition. "As soon as the train stops, the EMS squad will come and transport you and your mother to the hospital. They will want to move quickly. Try to stay calm. For now, why don't you come with me to pack the suitcases? Hilda and Harry will make sure the suitcases get to the hospital and also handle Skippy's trip to the animal spa. Your mother is very proud of you, Paula. I wish you and your mother the very best. It's been a pleasure knowing you," Dr. Waters said.

Jane and Alex were the ambulance staff. They were very nice but all business. I could not believe how quickly they got us to the hospital. I had never experienced driving so fast and hearing such a loud siren noise. They had a lot of equipment attached to Mom. I tried to comfort Mom as best I could.

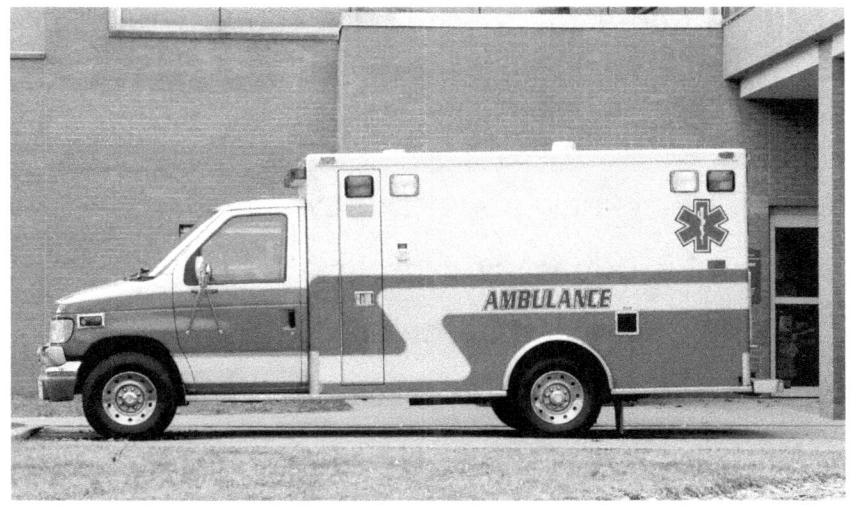

What Do You Want on Your Pancakes?

People in the emergency room were expecting us. They took Mom to an exam room right away. I was asked to stay in the waiting room. A social worker by the name of Dean Rush came to be with me. He knew all about what had gone on. Dean reminded me of my Uncle Ronnie, the professional comedian. He was easy to talk with. Dean promised to keep me informed about my mother. "As soon as they have completed her exam, I will get you back to see her. I am sure you are worried. You have every right to be," he said. Dean knew about Skippy and shared a little bit about his Doberman pinscher, Rex.

Talking with Dean helped get my mind off thinking about Mom. He asked about the work I did at Aunt Jenn's pet store. He also asked me what I thought about the dog food he was giving to Rex. We also talked a lot about Sherman. I did most of the talking. With everything that had gone on, I forgot how much I missed and cared for Sherman.

After what seemed like forever, a nurse came to get Dean and me. We were taken into an exam room. Mom was over the moon to see me. Two doctors were waiting by her bed. The doctors had already spoken to Mom. The test results showed that Mom was suffering from a large ulcer. She had been having stomach pain for almost a year but just thought it was bad indigestion. She had not told anyone about it. The doctors said she would need surgery as soon as possible to repair the damage to her stomach. At that moment, I felt like fainting.

Mom said, "Listen, Paula, everything is going to be just fine. Dean will explain more about what is going to happen next. Right now, I need to rest before going to surgery." I could not really hug her very well because of all the tubes that were hooked up to her. But we held hands, and she told me how much she loved me.

What Do You Want on Your Pancakes?

Dean took me to a private room. He explained about mom's condition. I had heard what the doctors said but really did not understand what everything meant. I was still worried. However, now I knew that it was not as serious as I had thought. Mom was going to need surgery to repair her ulcer. She would also need to watch what she ate, avoiding spicy food, rich sauces, and greasy things like bacon. They thought she would be in the hospital for about two days.

I liked having Dean with me. But I felt like I was being babysat. I started having one of those "you need to grow up" moments. I said to myself, *You are twenty-two years old, Paula, and need to start acting your age.* Then I wondered if Aunt Jenn was sending Sherman so he could babysit me. I did not think so but was not entirely sure.

Anyhow, Sherm—that's what I call him—is my pal, and we really do love one another. Like most couples, we have our ups and downs.

He is my biggest cheerleader and encourages me not to worry so much about things I cannot control. When he helps me out it is usually because I need it. We help one another. So no, I do not think he babies me.

QUESTIONS/THOUGHTS

- Does anyone baby you? How do you like it?
- What does it feel like to be in love?
- Have you ever had help from a social worker, psychologist, or counselor?

After two hours of waiting, the surgeon came to talk with Dean and me. Her name was Dr. Reardon, but she told us we could call her Dr. Gail. I could not help thinking maybe there had been a problem with the surgery. When Dr. Gail opened her mouth, I froze like a popsicle.

"Your mother is going to be fine. She will need to stay in the hospital another day or so and then will need to rest and recover for four to six weeks. I know you are not from here, so Dean will help plan how to get back home. Any questions?" she asked.

Dr. Gail did not have much time for questions, but she thought my mom would be just fine. My mind was going a mile a minute. I asked two or three quick questions then thanked Dr. Gail for helping my mother. My mind then turned to what would happen next.

I called Aunt Jenn to give her an update on Mom's condition, only to discover that Dean had already called her with an update. Once again, I felt like I was being treated like a child. I told Jenn that I had a few ideas of my own about what the next steps might be. She sounded surprised. I asked if she would be willing to come to Minneapolis and fly home with Mom and Skippy. I told her I would like to go on to Chicago by train with Sherman to enjoy the rest of my vacation in Chicago.

"I think that sounds like a plan, Paula. I will check flights to Minneapolis and try to come as soon as possible. I will also try and figure out how to transfer your mom's train ticket over to Sherman, if that is okay with you," she said. I could tell my aunt was proud of me for speaking up for myself. She did not say that in so many words, but I could just tell.

My phone was ringing. It was Sherman. He had arrived at the airport. "It is so good to hear your voice," I told him.

"I am really happy to be here," he said.

We got caught up and then decided he would take an Uber to the hospital. I could not wait to give him a great big hug.

Mom had a private room. She was not really herself. I understood it was because of the pain medication and having just come back from the surgery recovery room. I tried to let her rest and not ask too many questions.

Before long, Sherman showed up. He had a beautiful vase of flowers for Mom. He said the flowers were from all her friends and family back in Spokane. Mom smiled and threw him a big kiss. Sherman told us how everyone was doing back home and said that they sent their love. Mom fell in and out of sleep.

Sherm and I went to the hospital cafeteria so he could get something to eat. He was starving. We agreed that I would stay with mom overnight and he would go back to the hotel. We were sooo happy to see each other. We talked about the next few days and tried to stay focused on what we could do to help Mom. We also talked a little about our upcoming time in Chicago but did not want to get ahead of ourselves.

I had been thinking about Skippy but not too much. Part of the reason was that I was thinking about Mom. The other reason was that it did not feel like I needed him so much to help calm my nerves. Maybe I had started to think of Skippy more as my dog than my helper dog. Time will tell. In any case, I was not worried about having him with me in Chicago. Who knows, maybe I am starting to grow up.

QUESTIONS/THOUGHTS

- Do you know anyone who has a service or helper dog?
- Has anyone ever told you to grow up or act your age?
- How do you think Paula and Sherman will get along in Chicago?
- What would you want to see and do if you were in Chicago?

After Sherm finished eating in the cafeteria, we decided it would be good for him to go back to the hotel. He had been traveling all day. I went to stay with Mom. She was awake but still tired. We talked about Aunt Jenn coming to get her and me going on to Chicago with Sherman. She thought both ideas made a lot of sense. Mom was very happy that I was going to have a real vacation. "I can always go to Chicago once I feel better. Who knows, I may even find myself a boyfriend, like you have, to go with me," she said with a big laugh. There was a nice pull-out bed in mom's room. It was pretty comfy.

While mom slept and was visited throughout the night by hospital staff, I went through my emails and thought back to when I was in school. I remember feeling alone and different, especially in high school. Most of my friends were other special education students. Many of the kids had been in my same class since elementary school. I had trouble learning. But I always got along with everybody.

I tried to be positive, although sometimes it was hard. Right now, I was feeling like I had a lot to offer. Everyone has strengths and weaknesses. The next thing I knew, my eyes were getting heavy. I said my prayers and off to sleep I went.

"Good morning, sunshine," my mom said in a happy voice. I asked how she felt. She reported having a good night's sleep, except for being woken up several times for medication and to have her vitals taken. Mom was smiling, which was a good sign. "I spoke with Aunt Jenn, and she will be arriving tomorrow to take me back home. Hopefully, I will be ready to travel the following day. She told me that you and Sherman are taking the train to Chicago and staying there for a few days. Sorry you will not have as much time there as we planned. I guess I put a monkey wrench in the plans. But it is great that you and Sherman will have some time to explore together," Mom said with a twinkle in her eye.

As much as I was worried about Mom, spending time with Sherman in Chicago made me happy just thinking about it. The doctors thought mom was healing well and was ready to fly home in a day or two. So, I did not feel too bad leaving her.

The following day Aunt Jenn arrived, a half hour before Sherm and I were to leave for the train station. We said our happy and sad goodbyes. Mom and Aunt Jenn were thrilled for Sherm and me. They kept telling us not to worry about them and that everything would be fine. Of course, I would worry, but I tried not to get too teary-eyed. I also told them to give Skippy a big hug for me.

Sherman and I had a wonderful time on our train ride to Chicago. He had never been on a train before. We held hands, looked at the scenery, and talked about what to do in Chicago. Luckily, we would have five full days in Chicago since we could fly home instead of taking the train.

What Do You Want on Your Pancakes?

The train company agreed to refund our money because of Mom's medical emergency. That was fine with me because I had already had a great train ride.

We finally arrived at Union Station in Chicago. It was a beautiful one-hundred-year-old building. Sherm and I took a taxi to the hotel where mom and I were going to stay. It was a very nice place and located close to places we wanted to visit in the city. After checking in, we went to one of the famous deep-dish pizza restaurants a few blocks from our hotel.

We had never been to a really big city, so it was fun seeing all the people hustle and bustle. Our server at the restaurant was a real character. His name was Rudolpho, and he had grown up in Chicago. Rudolpho made suggestions about what to order. We went for the large deep-dish sausage pizza and a small Caesar salad to share. Rudolpho thought we would probably have leftover pizza for later that night or tomorrow morning.

The pizza took a half an hour to cook, so we had time to ask Rudolpho about places to go and see. He was full of great information.

Dinner was amazing. Sherm and I really enjoyed our meal and ended up eating way too much. During our walk back to the hotel, we stopped at a few stores that were still open. Our hotel room was big and had two queen-size beds. We were both tired from the trip and huge dinner. We were also extremely happy to be with one another.

QUESTIONS/THOUGHTS

- Have you ever ridden a train before?
- Have you ever had deep-dish pizza before?
- What would you want to do and see in Chicago?
- Where do you think the relationship between Paula and Sherman is going?

The next few days seemed to fly by. Sherm and I had a great time and really got along well together. We disagreed about some things but not many. I was surprised by how little I worried. I checked on mom and Skippy a lot. They were getting along great and were excited that I was having a wonderful vacation— finally. Sherm and I went to the Art Institute of Chicago, Navy Pier, the Sears Tower, and the Museum of Science and Industry. We took a boat ride on the Chicago River to view all the beautiful buildings in the city. We loved walking along Michigan Avenue and seeing the wonderful stores. Every night we tried a different type of restaurant. One night we saw the play *The Devil Wears Prada*. We loved the music and dancing of this production. Every day we went walking and sightseeing and enjoyed being together. This vacation turned out to be one of the best decisions I ever made.

On our last morning in Chicago, before taking a taxi to the airport, Sherm asked me to close my eyes.

We were sitting across from each other in the hotel restaurant having breakfast. The next thing I knew, he was putting a necklace around my neck. "Okay, you can open now," he said. I could not believe my eyes. He had bought me the most beautiful heart-shaped diamond necklace I had ever seen. I was speechless. I got up out of my chair and gave him the biggest hug and kiss ever. What a spectacular end to our vacation!

By the way, this was the vacation I was forced to take. I have come a long way and am just starting to reach my stride. I do believe the best is yet to come, and I am ready and eager to take the ride.

QUESTIONS/THOUGHTS

- What does being in love mean to you?
- Have you ever had Greek food?
- How do you solve disagreements with others?
- How long has it been since your last vacation?
- Where do you want to go on your next vacation?

**FOR FUN ACTIVITIES RELATED TO OUR STORIES,
USE THE QR CODE PROVIDED.**

Leo and Lucy

I DREAM

I am lying on the beach. The sun is shining on my belly and I feel very warm. When I open my eyes, I see very bright yellow stripes. The sun is blinding me. The sea is roaring. I can feel the sand between my toes. I hear a loud purr. I wonder if it's the engine of a ship. I'm tired and don't look to see where the sound is coming from. I enjoy the sun and play with my fingers in the sand. From time to time, I find a shell in the sand. The purring becomes louder. I feel something wet on my face. Are those raindrops?

MY DREAM IS OVER

Slowly I wake up. In my mind I am still on the beach. But when I open my eyes, Leo is standing in front of my face. He purrs as loud as a sawmill. With his rough tongue he licks my nose. I am sleepy. I want to go back to my dream. I don't want to get up yet. I pull the blanket over my face. Now Leo rests his paw on my mouth and licks my hair.

I say, "Leo, leave me alone, I want to sleep."

Leo doesn't care. He seems hungry. He meows and tries to crawl under my blanket. Now I feel his wet tongue on my toes. There, where I have just felt the sand. The wonderful feeling I had while dreaming comes back for a moment.

I hear something scratching on the door of my room. Now the door opens and with one leap Lucy jumps to Leo on my bed. She crawls up me and meows directly into my ear.

I turn around and meow back. If only they could understand me and finally get off my bed! But they are far too frisky and I know I won't be able to sleep anymore.

QUESTIONS/THOUGHTS

- Do you sometimes remember what you dreamed about after waking up?
- If so, what was your funniest dream?
- If so, what was your scariest dream?

I LIE IN BED AND DREAM WITH OPEN EYES

Leo and Lucy are my cats. They are siblings and four months old. At first, I wanted to have only one cat. But when I picked up Leo from the farm, Lucy meowed bitterly. It sounded as if a baby was crying. Then I took her too, because they were both so cute. I can understand Lucy. I would also not like to be separated from my favorite brother. So just like that, my adventure being a first-time pet owner got twice as exciting! And expensive!

The two of them always romp wildly through my apartment. Under the table, on the windowsill, and into my curtains. Sometimes I find them in the laundry basket. Leo and Lucy like to cuddle on my fresh laundry. They sleep between my sweaters and socks. Then there is always a lot of cat hair on my clothes. And I have to wash the laundry again.

Leo and Lucy

I don`t want Leo and Lucy to be bored in my apartment, so I make toys for them. For example, a mouse made of wool with a little bell around its neck. I don't know what I was worried about! Leo and Lucy play together often. Lucy likes to hide behind the cupboard with a toy. Leo will sneak up on her with his tail twitching. With one leap, he jumps on Lucy and takes the toy away from her. Or he tries to catch her tail with his paw. It is so funny when a toy makes a noise and they get in the ready position to pounce! I spend a lot of time watching them play.

QUESTIONS/THOUGHTS
- How do you like the names of the cats (Lucy and Leo)?
- If you had a cat, what would you call it?
- Have you ever watched cats play together? What was it like?

MY DAYDREAM IS INTERRUPTED

I hear a loud crackling sound. My thoughts are back in reality. Leo and Lucy are lying on the floor next to my bed. They purr contentedly and lick their mouths with their tongues. What happened? What were they doing while I was daydreaming? Why are they suddenly so calm and content? Now I discover the empty popcorn bag on my night table. I can't believe it, they have eaten my leftover popcorn! I scolded Leo and Lucy: "What stupid things you do! popcorn is not good for you. It's not cat food." They just look at me with a satisfied smile and lick their mouths with pleasure.

I don't usually have popcorn on my nightstand, but it's one of my guilty pleasures now that I live alone. On the weekends, I like to watch scary movies while cuddling in bed with a salty snack. My parents never let me eat in my room when I lived with them. I knew when I started living on my own there were some changes I was going to make. If my parents were here right now they would be saying, "I told you so!" I try not to think about that. Right now I need to make sure my cats are OK. Thank goodness a quick search on my phone tells me popcorn isn't toxic. And that's a good thing. I don't have the extra money in my bank account for two vet bills!

QUESTIONS/THOUGHTS

- What is your favorite movie snack?
- Do you have an emergency fund for possible expenses?
- Are there things you do at home that family would tell you not to do?

I CAN'T DREAM ANYMORE

I get up and go to the kitchen. In the kitchen I open a can of cat food. Immediately Leo and Lucy come into the kitchen. They know the sound of the can opener and always come running when they hear it. They know exactly when I prepare something for them. They sneak around my legs and purr again. Now they act as if nothing has happened.

Taking care of Leo and Lucy is sometimes not so easy. It is a lot of work. I have to clean their litter box. I have to buy food for them and take them to the vet. This means I have to watch what I spend and can't buy every new game and CD that gets released. I have to tidy up my apartment after they have their wild play in my living room. My best friends Bill and Emma were skeptical about me getting a cat. They thought I wouldn't take care of an animal properly. Since I live in my own apartment, I can decide for myself. The fun that I have with the two cats rewards me for all the work I have to do for them.

Leo and Lucy also give me a lot of love. When I watch them play with their toys my heart feels very warm. Cuddling with them and feeling their rough tongue on my skin when they lick me makes my heart jump. It was the best decision to bring the two of them home with me. I'm sure my friends Bill and Emma will think so soon too.

QUESTIONS/THOUGHTS

- How do you feel when animals are around you?
- Did you ever decide something someone else did not approve of?

PLANS FOR THE DAY

While Leo and Lucy are eating their proper cat food, I look up the plan for today on my calendar. It is Sunday, so I don`t have to go to work. I see nothing in my notes for today, but then I remember that my friends Bill and Emma called me yesterday and wanted to come over this afternoon for some cake and coffee.

That will be fun. It is nice out, and we can sit on the terrace. My friend Bill said he was going to make my favorite cake and bring it over.

Before my friends come to visit, I will have to tidy up my apartment. My laundry is lying on the floor in my bedroom and Lucy and Leo begin playing with a pair of socks. Also, after dinner last night I was too tired to do the washing up. I decide to do those jobs first and have a nice bath afterward as a treat.

Lucy and Leo are roaming around the bathroom while I'm lying in my bubble bath. They don't like water, but they love to play with the foam.

They nudge it with their nose and try to catch the foam between their paws. The bubbles burst and the cats look surprised. Watching the cats play with the foam is the most fun I have while having a bath.

QUESTIONS/THOUGHTS
- What is your favorite cake?
- What do you do before someone comes to visit you?

SUNSHINE IN MY FACE AGAIN

My front doorbell rings. Lucy and Leo trot slowly to the door. "Let's see who's coming," I say to the two. They sneak around my legs and meow. "Hello, Bill and Emma. I'm so happy you're here. I have set the table on the terrace, if you want to head that way," I say to my friends when they come through the door.

My friend Bill puts his famous strawberry cake on the table. Lucy and Leo scurry around the table legs in excitement. "Be good, and don't jump on the table," I reprimand. They look at me with their big eyes and send me a pleading look. I remain strict and stare back. Lucy and Leo give up and lie down together on a chair. They curl up and put their heads on the cushion of the chair, and it looks like they are listening to us while we talk.

I sit back, enjoy the taste of the fresh strawberries in my mouth, and take pleasure in the rays of sunshine on my face. The sun on my face takes me back to my dream this morning. Only the sand between my toes is missing. What a lovely Sunday!

QUESTIONS/THOUGHTS

- Everything seems to be perfect for the leading character in the story.
- What fatal moment could happen next to them?

THE FATAL MOMENT

After each of us has eaten a delicious piece of strawberry cake with cream, we sit on the terrace and talk about what happened in our lives within the last week. Leo and Lucy have fallen asleep on the chair and are purring loudly. I feel very relaxed. After the sun has disappeared behind clouds, we slowly clear the table and go inside.

Together with my friend Bill, I do the dishes in the kitchen and shout to my friend Emma that she should bring the cats inside and make sure to close the terrace door.

While I wash the plates, Leo strokes back and forth between my legs and meows. I almost fall over and let a plate skip from my hand.

"Leo, you have to be careful. The kitchen is no playground. Why don't you go into the living room and play with your woolly mouse together with Lucy?" I say. Leo doesn't listen to what I say and continues to stroke back and forth between my legs. Now he scratches me very gently on the leg. I am alarmed and the plate from my hand falls into the dishwater, but luckily it doesn't break. "What's wrong with him?" my friend Bill asks.

Now the kitchen door also slams loudly due to a gust of wind. An eerie thought comes to my mind. "Emma, did you close the terrace door?" I shout loudly through the closed kitchen door. "And is Lucy with you?" I ask in an anxious tone. "Oh no," is the only answer I get. I cannot believe my friend left the door open and didn't look after Lucy properly. What a foolish thing to do!

Now everything happens very quickly. I give my friend Bill a bag of cat treats and send him with it to the street in front of the house.

The familiar shaking sound is supposed to attract cats. My friend Emma says, "I'll stay inside, watch Leo, and ring the bell of the mouse toy very loudly. Maybe that will attract Lucy." I myself take an open can of cat food to entice Lucy with smell. Then I go to the garden and call out loud for Lucy.

Desperately I run through the garden calling for my beloved cat. Leo and Lucy have never run away. They love it around the apartment and always stay near me. Why did my friend Emma not close the door behind her? She has concerns that I can't take care of a cat, but she is the one who lost Lucy! Hopefully Lucy will quickly find her way back to us. Many bad imaginations go through my head:

Lucy alone on a street with many cars.

Lucy looking for food in a garbage can.

Lucy in a fight with a big dog.

How beautiful was my daydream of the beach this morning in comparison?

QUESTIONS/THOUGHTS

- Where could Lucy be?
- Have you ever had a pet run away?

TOGETHER AT LEAST

My friend Bill calls me on my cell. He says that Lucy is not to be seen. He has already rung the doorbells of the neighbors and asked every person he saw on the street. My desperation increases. I have no idea what else I can do. Panic does not help me now.

I sit down on a chair on the terrace and think. Where do Lucy and Leo like to play? What do they like to play? Where could Lucy be hiding? Where could she have locked herself in?

Now the tool shed in the neighbor's garden comes into my mind. My neighbor told me that a family of mice has nested there. I quickly walk through the neighboring gardens toward the shed. As I get closer, I hear meowing.

Indeed, Lucy sits in front of the tool shed and sniffs with her nose at the bottom of the door crack. She paws on the ground. Slowly I approach and speak her name softly. I hear a soft squeak from inside the tool shed. I put the opened can of cat food on the ground and call Lucy again. She doesn't seem to be interested in me or the food. Carefully I stroke her back and take her into my arms.

I walk Lucy back inside and close the door. My friend Emma has tears in her eyes and apologizes to me for leaving Lucy outside. We say our goodbyes, and I feel exhausted. Still holding Lucy, she purrs and looks at me, a little puzzled. She can't imagine how worried I was. With a sigh, I let myself sink into my living room armchair and look out the window to my terrace. Lucy is on my lap. What a day! I think to myself: A lot of responsibility can also mean a lot of worries. That is for sure.

QUESTIONS/THOUGHTS

- Do you agree with the sentence: "A lot of responsibility can also mean a lot of worries"?
- Did our main character prove she can be a responsible pet owner?

FOR FUN ACTIVITIES RELATED TO OUR STORIES,
USE THE QR CODE PROVIDED.

Best Friends Forever

"EVIE," MY MOM HOLLERED up the stairs to my bedroom, "it's time to get up! We have a big day today!"

"Big day?" I wondered. Today was Saturday. So what was the big hurry?

"Okay, Mom! I'll be down for breakfast in five," I answered her.

My name is Evie and even though I just turned twenty years old, I still love all things Disney. I even have a Disney t-shirt for every day of the week. Since it was Saturday, I pulled my teal-blue Ariel shirt out of the drawer and put it on.

What Do You Want on Your Pancakes?

Every Saturday, it's the teal-blue Ariel shirt. Sunday is the pink Minnie Mouse shirt, which is my favorite.

Then I quickly made my bed. I make my bed first thing after I get dressed in the morning. It starts my day off right, and I just love my new Disney Princess comforter with matching pillows. I know people who see absolutely no point in making their beds in the morning. Honestly, I don't understand them. How can anyone begin their day knowing their bed was a messy pile of sheets and blankets? Not me!

My next stop was the bathroom, where I brushed by teeth and did my hair. I have a mop of curly red hair, and sometimes it hurts to brush it through to get the tangles out. On those days, I just pull it all up in a scrunchy and call it a day. Today was one of those days.

Finally, exactly five minutes later, I bounded down the stairs into the kitchen, shouting, "What's for breakfast, Mom?"

I ask that question every day, even though I know the answer. Breakfast is cornflakes. And a banana and a glass of orange juice, no pulp. It always has to be the same for me. You see, I am on the autism spectrum, and I get really upset when we run out of cornflakes and I have to have something else for breakfast. It makes me feel good to know exactly what to expect every day, and if things change, I might just have a meltdown.

QUESTIONS/THOUGHTS

- Do you have your own morning routine?
- If so, what is it?
- What is your favorite breakfast?
- Do you make your bed?
- Every day? Sometimes? Never?

"Are you up for a surprise today?" asked Mom.

Oh no, not a surprise. I hated surprises. On Saturday after cornflakes, a banana, and orange juice, Mom and I go for a walk in the park. That's just what we did on Saturday. No surprises for me!

"We are going to make a quick stop at my friend Miss Barb's house before we go to the park. I hope you don't mind, Evie," said Mom.

Miss Barb was my mom's best friend. They had known each other since they were in third grade. That was a long time to be friends. Because I have autism, it is hard for me to make friends. I wish I had a friend like Miss Barb, but more my age of course.

I liked Miss Barb's house. It was small and cozy, and she always had a vase of fresh flowers from her garden on the kitchen table. She had two dogs. One was a yellow Chihuahua named Candy, who was kind of crazy and barked at anything that moved, which sometimes gave me a headache.

Her other dog was a great big black Labrador retriever named Bear. He was a special dog who had special training, and she called him her therapy dog. I don't know why Miss Barb needed a therapy dog, but I do know I always felt better after a visit with the Bear.

I don't know exactly how or why Bear made me feel better, but he did. Bear didn't bark like Candy the Chihuahua did. He didn't jump up on you and lick your face because he was glad to see you. Bear was just, well, THERE.

What Do You Want on Your Pancakes?

I remember one afternoon after my mom picked me up from work and we stopped to see Miss Barb. I worked in the kitchen at the New Day Café. My job was to roll the silverware up in napkins, which were used in setting the tables. I loved my job. I was good at it. Mr. Beasley, my boss, complimented me on what a good job I did and that made me feel proud.

Anyway, on this particular day, everything was going good, and I went on my afternoon break like I always do. When I came back and started rolling silverware again, I noticed that the knives and forks were all dirty! I panicked. I looked for clean knives and forks, but there were none to be found. Mr. Beasley stuck his head in the kitchen door and hollered, "Evie, let's move it! We need to set up the tables for the dinner rush!" Now I was in total meltdown mode, and I started to cry. I looked up to see Timmy, the dishwasher, who I used to think was kind of cute, pointing at me and laughing!

To make matters worse, a few of the other kitchen workers were laughing at me too. I didn't tell my mom about it later that afternoon when she picked me up. I didn't want to talk about it. But as I sat in the front seat of our old Volvo, my hands were still balled up in tight fists and my throat hurt from holding back tears. I think the worst part was that I had thought up till then that the folks I worked with were my friends.

What Do You Want on Your Pancakes?

When we got to Miss Barb's house, she and my mom immediately headed for the kitchen and got into a big discussion about the bake sale they were planning at the library. Silently, I sat down in one of the wooden armchairs in Miss Barb's dining room. Still fighting back tears, I started to practice the special breathing that I had learned from my therapist, but it wasn't working. I thought for sure I was headed for another total meltdown.

I didn't even notice when Bear, Miss Barb's therapy dog, walked quietly into the room. He came right over to me, laid his head in my lap, and looked up into my eyes. It was like he could read my mind. Without even thinking about it, I relaxed my balled up fists and started stroking his head. My breathing slowed down. Before I knew it, I had calmed down. Bear looked up at me, a kind of goofy grin on his face, and slowly wagged his tail. That was the day I started to understand what made therapy dogs special.

QUESTIONS/THOUGHTS

- Have you ever had a meltdown?
- If so, what caused it?
- Have you ever met a therapy dog?
- Have people ever made fun of you?
- How did you react?

That was almost a year ago. And today, on a Saturday, my mom and I were headed to Miss Barb's for a quick visit before we made our regular Saturday trip to the park. I was busy thinking about the new climbing-wall feature there that I wanted to try out when I my thoughts were interrupted by Miss Barb's voice. "Hey there, Earth to Evie! Did you hear what I just said? Let's go around to the backyard. There's someone there I want you to meet."

Oh great, I thought. Meeting new people was not my favorite thing to do. But when we opened the gate and walked into Miss Barb's backyard, there were no new people there to meet.

Instead, Bear was sitting there with another dog I had never seen before. The new dog was different from any other dog I had ever seen. None of his parts seemed to fit together. He was tall and gangly. His legs were furry, skinny stilts. It looked like he could get tangled up in them. His ears were too long for his head, and they flopped from side to side when he walked. His fur was a mass of wavy white and tan splotches, and his pink tongue seemed to hang down almost to the ground. His nose was long and narrow and came to a bit of a point. Underneath two amazingly furry eyebrows were the saddest eyes I had ever seen.

"Evie, I'd like you to meet Jerry. Jerry, this is my friend Evie," said Miss Barb.

Jerry, Miss Barb and my mom went on to tell me, had been enrolled in the same canine therapy program that her Bear had graduated from. Jerry's training to be a therapy dog had been going well. He was friendly and calm, he knew all his basic commands, and he walked nicely on a leash. But there was one thing Jerry just would not do. He refused to walk over to someone and put his head in their lap, which was really important when a therapy dog visits patients in the hospital or people in a nursing home. His trainers tried and tried, but Jerry just would not do it. That's how Jerry became a "career-change dog." Which meant that instead of being a therapy dog, Jerry's new career was going to be as a family pet.

"So, Evie," my mom said, "I was thinking, if it's alright with you, that we could be Jerry's foster family."

Jerry seemed to be smiling at me. "What does that mean, be his foster family?"

"It means Jerry would come to live with us while the Therapy Dog Organization finds him a forever home. We will take care of him until then. We will feed him, and take him on walks, play ball with him in the backyard, give him a bath if he needs one—all that stuff," Mom explained.

"Jeez, Mom, that sounds like a lot of work to me! I've never had a pet before, not even a goldfish! I don't know if I could handle it."

But when I looked over at Jerry, he was still smiling at me. "Well, okay, I guess. If you think it's a good idea, we could try being a foster family for a while, anyway." And with those words, I heard a thump, thump, thump. It was Jerry, wagging his supersized tail.

Best Friends Forever

We never did make it to the park that day. On the way home, Jerry sat in the back seat with me. I was nervous that he'd try to sit in my lap or lick my face, but not Jerry. He just sat on his side of the back seat, spending half the time looking out the window and half the time looking at me, all the while with that goofy grin on his face. His eyes didn't look so sad anymore.

Over the next week, I got to know Jerry better, and he got to know me.

Jerry would sit and watch me every morning first thing when I made my bed. I was afraid he might jump up on my Disney princess comforter, but not Jerry. He was happy to sleep in his doggy bed next to mine.

I walked him every morning before breakfast, and on Monday I ran into Olivia, who was a regular lunch customer at the New Day Café, walking her dog, a golden retriever named Maddie. Maddie and Jerry seemed to like walking together, so Olivia and I started meeting every morning at 7:30 and walking together too.

What Do You Want on Your Pancakes?

Jerry's breakfast was always the same, just like my cornflakes, banana, and orange juice, no pulp. His breakfast was two cups of kibble though.

Jerry sat at the front door every morning and watched me hop into the front passenger seat of the Volvo when Mom drove me to work. When I came home from work in the afternoon, there was Jerry, sitting in the same spot as he was in the morning. I don't think he sat there all day waiting for me, but it would be kind of cool if he did. I really looked forward to seeing him there, waiting for me every day when I got home from the restaurant. Even if it had been a tough day at work, seeing Jerry waiting for me at the door every day never failed to put a smile on my face.

QUESTIONS/THOUGHTS

- Do you have a pet?
- How does your pet make you feel?
- Evie and Olivia have become friends. Tell us about one of your friends.

On Saturday morning at breakfast my mom said, "Hey, Evie, what do you say we go to the park today? We never did get there last week."

"Okay, great! But can we bring Jerry?" I answered between mouthfuls of cornflakes. "I really want to try climbing that new rock wall!"

The park was exactly a mile and a half from our house, and the parking lot was only about half full, which was good, because I don't like crowds.

As I got out of the car with Jerry on his leash, I heard a voice from across the lot. "Hey, Evie! What are YOU doing here?" It was Olivia, being pulled by Maddie, the golden retriever, across the parking lot in our direction.

"Hey, Olivia!" I said. "We come here almost every Saturday. Today I really want a try climbing the rock wall."

My mom had a big smile on her face as she asked, "Evie, do you want to introduce me to your friend?"

"Oh, uh, yeah, Mom." I hadn't really thought of Olivia as my friend, but I guess she was, right?

"Mom, this is Olivia and her dog, Maddie. We call her Maddie the Maniac because she is overly exuberant. Olivia and Maddie walk with me and Jerry every morning, and Olivia eats lunch at the New Day Café a lot, too."

We headed over to the rock wall together. It was higher than I thought it would be. Olivia took one look at it and said, "Sorry, Evie. You can count me out. I'm afraid of heights!"

I handed Jerry's leash over to Mom. "Okay, well, here goes nothing." I took a deep breath and stepped up to the wall.

Now, what I was about to do was not really rock climbing. Rock climbing is when you climb real cliffs and mountainsides using ropes and a harness, and grab onto real rocks on the way up. Bouldering is rock climbing up an artificial wall with carefully placed hand- and footholds, without using ropes or a harness.

Bouldering is not as difficult as real rock climbing, but it's not easy, either.

Mom had taken me to an indoor rock climbing place twice over the past year, so I had some experience with bouldering. But this wall was much higher than that one.

Okay. I took a deep breath and stepped onto the first foothold. You have to remember to use your toes to get the best traction on the footholds.

You also have to use your legs to push yourself up, because if you try to use your arms to pull yourself up, your arms will get tired and you'll never make it to the top.

I was making pretty good progress, doing everything right and remembering to keep my hips close to the wall and not let them sag out and drag me down. I focused on each foothold and hand grip, one at a time, slowly, carefully climbing to the top of the wall. Before I knew it, I was there! I MADE IT! I heard Mom and Olivia cheering and looked down to see them waving and Jerry wagging his tail as if he understood.

QUESTIONS/THOUGHTS

- Climbing the rock wall was a challenge that Evie was able to overcome. What challenges have you faced in your life?
- Were you able to overcome your challenges?
- If so, how?
- Olivia is afraid of heights. What are you afraid of?

Funny thing about rock climbing, though. Once you get to the top of the wall, you have to climb back down. And that is even harder than climbing up because you are tired and more likely to make a misstep and fall. Carefully, I retraced my steps as I climbed back down the wall. I had made it about halfway down when disaster struck. I put my toes down to where a foothold was supposed to be, and there was nothing. I tried to hold myself up just with my arms, but I couldn't hold on. I fell.

Next thing I knew, I was lying in the sand at the bottom of the rock wall. My head felt fine. I tried bending my arms and legs. Good. Everything worked. I sat up.

"We've got to get you to the first-aid station, quickly!" I heard my mother say.

"Why? I'm fine!" I answered.

I looked down at my knee and saw what she was talking about. I must have smacked my knee pretty hard on the wall on the way down, and it was a bloody mess.

A crowd had started to form around us. Everybody was looking at me. All I could think about was that I might need stitches. I was scared to death and started to hyperventilate, which happens when I have a meltdown. It's like I can't take a deep breath no matter how hard I try. And the harder I try, the worse it gets.

I was struggling to breathe when I saw Jerry walking calmly toward me through the crowd. He looked at me with his goofy grin, and then he did it. He walked right over to me and PUT HIS HEAD IN MY LAP! I felt my body relax as I stroked his head. Soon, my breathing was back to normal. Sure, my knee was still a bloody mess, and I might need stitches, but I could get through this. I could get through it because Jerry would be with me. Jerry, the foster dog I wasn't even sure I wanted at first. Jerry, who helped me make my first friend. Jerry, who waited at the door for me to come home from work every day.

Jerry, the dog who failed therapy-dog training because he refused to put his head in patients' laps. Jerry, lying right now with his head in MY lap, looking up at me with that goofy grin.

I could see two emergency medical technicians from the first-aid station running in our direction. I looked over at my mom and Olivia and said, "Don't worry. I'll be okay. But Mom…"

"Yes, Evie," she responded.

"Can we please keep Jerry?"

The smile on Mom's face was almost as goofy as Jerry's. And then I realized I was smiling too.

QUESTIONS/THOUGHTS

- Have you ever hurt yourself like Evie does in the story?
- What did you think when Jerry put his head in Evie's lap?
- Jerry has a goofy grin. Can you make one?

**FOR FUN ACTIVITIES RELATED TO OUR STORIES,
USE THE QR CODE PROVIDED.**

I Can Do It

I HATE CHANGE. I am perfectly happy with my life and want it to stay exactly the way it is. And this is the way it is.

My name is Evie Dawson and I am twenty-two years old. I live with my mother in Leland, North Carolina. I was diagnosed with Level 1 autism spectrum disorder (ASD) when I was four years old.

My sister Kate graduated from high school this past June and just started college this past September. She is a freshman at the University of North Carolina in Wilmington.

During the week, she lives in a dormitory on campus, but she comes home almost every weekend to wash all her dirty clothes and, according to our mom, "eat us out of house and home."

Mom works during the day, and so I have two aides who come to stay with me while she's working: Monica in the morning and Karen in the afternoon until mom gets home from work. That worked out just fine. Fine, that is, until Monica had to go and have a baby. Then, everything changed. And not in a good way.

QUESTIONS/THOUGHTS
- How do you deal with change in your life?
- Do you live at home with your family? How is that working out?
- Do you have support staff? What do they help you with?

After Monica announced that she was taking something called maternity leave to have her baby, we all sat down at the dining room table to have a family meeting to figure out what we were going to do. Mom's first thought was to find someone to replace Monica in the mornings, but the agency didn't currently have anyone available for that time slot.

"Mom," I said, "I can handle things by myself in the morning until Karen gets here at one o'clock."

What Do You Want on Your Pancakes?

Neither my mom nor my sister seemed convinced. But since there didn't seem to be any other solution to the problem, Mom agreed to try out my plan for a week and see how things went.

On Monday, Mom left for her shift at the hospital, where she is a nurse, at 6:30 a.m. as usual. I was still asleep. When my alarm clock went off at 8:00 a.m., I reached over, half asleep, and turned it off. When Karen arrived at 1:00 p.m., I was still in bed, sound asleep. It was already afternoon and I hadn't even gotten dressed, eaten breakfast, made my bed, or taken my dog Jerry out for his morning walk. My plan was not off to a good start.

Tuesday started off a little better. Mom was sure to wake me up before she left for work. Unfortunately, I never got any farther than the kitchen. I poured myself a bowl of cornflakes, sat down at the kitchen table, and that's where things went wrong. I made the mistake of turning on the kitchen TV to the Disney Channel.

I Can Do It

I should mention that I have been obsessed with all things Disney since we visited Disney World when I was five. We have gone every year since. Anyway, when I turned on the Disney Channel Tuesday morning, I found myself in the middle of a *Hannah Montana* marathon, featuring one of my all-time favorites, Miley Cyrus! Before I knew it, there was a knock on the door. It was Karen, my afternoon aide. It was one o'clock! I was still in my pajamas, my bed was unmade, and my poor dog Jerry was still waiting for me to take him on his morning walk.

Mom was not happy, but I talked her into giving me another chance. On Wednesday Mom made sure I was up before she left for work. She patiently went through the list of things I had to do: eat breakfast, brush my teeth, get dressed, and take Jerry for his morning walk. I stood at the door and gave her a big thumbs up as she drove away to work. As soon as Mom was gone, I sprang into action! No television for me this morning.

I ate a bowl of cornflakes, washed it down with a glass of orange juice, and loaded my dirty dishes into the dishwasher. I stood back and admired the clean kitchen before heading to my bathroom, where I brushed my teeth and even flossed for good measure! I was on a roll! Stepping into my bedroom, I made my bed and carefully arranged my Disney Princess pillows. I know I am twenty-two years old, but you're never too old for the Disney Princesses, are you?

I love them all, but Ariel has always been my favorite, maybe because we both have red hair. Anyway, next I got dressed for the day: jeans and a sweatshirt, since it mid-March and still a little cool outside. At the back door, I grabbed Jerry's leash from its hook. Magically, he appeared at my side, smiling his lopsided grin and looking up at me expectantly with his big brown eyes. Off we went for our morning walk, and it was only 10:00 a.m.! I was doing great!

Jerry and I walked over to Greenfield Park, which was one of his favorite places to go. There were always lots of children and other dogs at Greenfield Park, and Jerry just loved that. I wanted to make up for the fact that I had forgotten about him for the past two days. While we were walking, I reached into my pocket for my phone and realized I had left it on the kitchen counter. Oh well, at least it wasn't lost again. When we arrived, there were a few children on the swings and even more over at the sandbox.

In the dog park area, I could see several dogs already romping and running about. Jerry had to introduce himself to each of the children before heading over to the dog park, where I waited and watched him play tag and fetch and wrestle with his four-legged friends.

QUESTIONS/THOUGHTS

- Do you have a dog or other pet?

What Do You Want on Your Pancakes?

- What are your responsibilities for taking care of your pet?
- Do you ever lose track of time or forget to do things?

I glanced at my watch: 11:30. Time to head home. I clipped the leash back on Jerry and led him out of the dog park. Then I heard a familiar voice. "Hey, Evie! I haven't seen you in like forever!" It was my friend Olivia and Maddie, her crazy golden retriever. Jerry barked a hello, and Maddie responded in kind. I ran over to Olivia and she gave me a hug.

"What have you been up to, girl?" she asked.

"Oh boy, wait until you hear what's going on with me," I responded. We found an empty bench and sat down to talk. We had a lot to catch up on, since we hadn't seen each other for awhile. It didn't seem that we had been talking all that long when I looked down at Jerry and noticed he was sound asleep and snoring. That made me check my watch. I did a double take.

It couldn't be 2:00! Liv and I couldn't possibly have been sitting here talking for over two hours. But we had. I had lost track of time.

I ran all the way home, dragging Jerry behind me. When I turned the corner to my street, I stopped short and let out a gasp. In our driveway I saw three cars: my helper Karen's VW bug, my mom's Honda, and a Leland police car! Oh no! Was I ever in trouble now! I stepped into the kitchen to find my mom, my aide Karen, and a very tall, very serious-looking policeman deep in conversation.

"Hi, Mom, I'm home," I said.

"Evie! Where have you been? Karen got here and there was no sign of you except for your phone on the kitchen counter. She looked around the neighborhood and then she called me at work. I had to leave an important meeting to rush home. We called the police, thinking something had happened to you. WHERE HAVE YOU BEEN?"

The policeman seemed like the only one who was glad to see me. My mom and Karen just seemed really, really angry. I felt terrible. I had given both of them an awful scare. I hung my head and started to cry.

QUESTIONS/THOUGHTS
- What kinds of things make you upset?
- Evie's reaction to being upset is to cry. How do you react when you are upset?

By that evening, we had all calmed down. My mother called another family meeting. My sister drove home from her college dorm and didn't look too happy as she sat down with us at the dining room table. Kate looked as if she felt almost as bad about this as I did. She gave me a reassuring hug as I felt warm tears rolling down my cheeks again.

"Well," Mom began, "we certainly had a lot of excitement in our day today, didn't we?"

"I'm so sorry for messing up again. All I do is cause trouble. I don't mean to, but I do. I get distracted. I lost track of time. AGAIN. I feel like such a failure," I sobbed.

Mom glared at me from across the table and began in an angry voice, "Now, you just listen to me, young lady…"

Oh no. I had heard that tone in her voice before. I squinched my eyes shut and waited for Mom to continue.

She was right to be mad. I was a disappointment. I was irresponsible. I was nothing but trouble. The tears leaked out of the corners of my eyes and continued to drip down my cheeks, forming a puddle in front of me on the dining room table.

The next thing I felt were my mother's hands on either side of my shoulders. She was standing in back of my chair. When she spoke, her voice was soft and soothing. "Evie," she began, "I want you to take a few deep breaths and calm down. You are not a failure or a troublemaker. And as far as you messing up, EVERYONE messes things up every once in a while. You are way too hard on yourself. Look at all you've accomplished in just three days this week. Every day you got better and better at being alone and living independently. Change doesn't happen overnight. It takes time and effort. Sometimes, like today, things don't go as well you wanted. But you can't give up. You have to keep trying. I am so proud of what you have accomplished so far!"

"That's right, Evie," Kate chimed in. "I'm proud of you too! Mom called me to come home tonight because both of us want to pitch in and help you to become more independent. We're here to help. So let's figure out how! But before we start, I think what we need right now is a big Dawson family group hug. What do you say?"

Kate and Mom pulled me out of my chair and we hugged each other tightly. A Dawson family group hug was just what I needed at that moment. I smiled through my tears. I wasn't a disappointment.

What Do You Want on Your Pancakes?

My family was proud of me, and that made me feel proud of myself. Change was hard, but I wasn't going to give up. And besides, it was only Wednesday! With the help of Mom and Kate, who knew how much I could accomplish before the week was over?

FOR FUN ACTIVITIES RELATED TO OUR STORIES, USE THE QR CODE PROVIDED.

Mrs. Smith

MY NAME IS DAVID. Every Monday I work until 4:00 p.m. Then, at 5:00 p.m. every Monday, I visit Mrs. Smith. Mrs. Smith is my neighbor, and she is a very nice neighbor indeed! I met Mrs. Smith for the first time when I was having what I call one of my Bad Days. On this particular Bad Day, I came home from work and could not open the door to my apartment. I could not find my key. I looked everywhere. The key was not in my bag. The key was not in my coat pocket. The key was not hanging around my neck on the keychain. Even under my doormat, I could not find my key.

What Do You Want on Your Pancakes?

When I met Mrs. Smith for the first time, I was sitting on my doormat feeling angry and lost. Instead of talking to me right away, she knelt down to me. I could hear her knees crack. Our heads were now at the same height. Mrs. Smith looked at me with her warm eyes. "What is wrong, my dear?" Mrs. Smith asked.

"I cannot find my key," I said to her.

"That is not a reason to make such a sad face. Come to my apartment and we will find a solution," Mrs. Smith said. This Bad Day when I first met Mrs. Smith was a Monday. Maybe it was not a Bad Day after all.

Mrs. Smith

QUESTIONS/THOUGHTS

- Have you ever lost your keys?
- Where do you usually keep your keys?
- Do you have neighbors?
- Are you friendly with your neighbors?

Mrs. Smith's apartment smells of grandmother. That's because Mrs. Smith is a grandmother. Unfortunately, she is not my grandmother. But I'm allowed to visit her every Monday anyway. We have a lot of fun together. Sometimes Mrs. Smith tells jokes that I don't understand. Mrs. Smith says that's no problem. She explains the jokes to me, and we have a good time laughing together. When Mrs. Smith laughs her belly bounces up and down because it is so big. After laughing at Mrs. Smith's jokes and bouncy belly, my belly aches like when I overdo it in an exercise class. Mrs. Smith says, "To laugh a lot is healthy." I think she is right. I always feel good when I am laughing.

I feel even better when I'm laughing together with someone else. Mrs. Smith talks a lot about her life. I listen to her. Sometimes I don't understand everything. I just nod my head and she tells stories about her life. She smiles a lot and says, "This is what life is like when you are old."

I don't know what life is like when you are old. When I do get old I want to tell stories about my life just like Mrs. Smith. That's why I have to remember what I'm doing now. And I have to experience many more things so I have lots of interesting stories to tell! When Mrs. Smith tells me stories about her life, she asks if I would like a snack. My favorite snack is Oreos. I usually take the two black cookies apart and then eat the white cream before eating the two black cookies. But Mrs. Smith buys Oreos especially for our visits most of the time. She knows what I like and don't like to eat.

Mrs. Smith

QUESTIONS/THOUGHTS

- Do you like Oreos? How do you eat them?
- Do you sometimes visit with people older than you? What are the visits like?
- Do you ever think about getting older yourself? What do you think that will be like?

Every Monday at 5:30 p.m., Mrs. Smith and I play Parcheesi. In this game, each player has four game pieces of the same color. You have to throw the dice and try to bring your game pieces all the way around the board to a safe home. If another player lands on the same square your piece is on, they send your piece back to start all over again! It can get quite nerve-wracking. Mrs. Smith and I really like to play Parcheesi. It is a very thrilling game. When we play, I always choose the blue game pieces. Blue reminds me of the ocean. I like the ocean, and it calms me down. Mrs. Smith always plays with the red game pieces. I don't know what red reminds her of.

Maybe I should ask her. Every game must have a winner and a loser. When I lose, I think, *Don't get mad. There's always the next time*. Then losing is not so bad.

QUESTIONS/THOUGHTS

- Do you like to play board games?
- Do you know the game Parcheesi, and do you like to play it?
- Which color game pieces would you choose, and what does the color remind you of?

Mrs. Smith

Today is Monday. I'm looking forward to playing Parcheesi. At 5:00 p.m. I'm ready to go ring Mrs. Smith's doorbell. While I am waiting, I can hear someone walking toward the door. I can also hear voices that I don't recognize behind Mrs. Smith's door. I ring the doorbell again. I can hear the sound of the bell. A voice from behind the door is coming closer. The door opens, but it's not Mrs. Smith standing in front of me. The woman at the door has brown hair and is wearing a skirt. "Hello, can I help you?" the woman asks.

Surprised, I stand speechless in the doorway, looking into the strange face. "Are you here to see Mrs. Smith?" the woman at the door asks.

I'm confused. Who is this woman? And where is my friend Mrs. Smith? Finally, I say to her, "Today is Monday. Every Monday I work until 4:00 p.m. Then, every Monday at 5:00 p.m., I come here to visit Mrs. Smith." The woman at the door explains to me that she is Mrs. Smith's daughter.

What Do You Want on Your Pancakes?

I still don't understand why she is standing in the doorway where Mrs. Smith usually stands every Monday. "Why are you standing in Mrs. Smith's doorway?" I ask her. The woman tells me that Mrs. Smith wasn't feeling very well this morning. She complained of pain in her heart. The ambulance had to come to take her to the hospital. And in the hospital, she passed away. "Why is Mrs. Smith gone? And where did she go?" I ask the woman in the door. I don't understand this. Mrs. Smith was here every Monday at 5:00 p.m. She never went away. Why should she go away? We always play Parcheesi together and laugh together and have a good time. But now, the woman in the doorway is telling me that Mrs. Smith is gone forever. She died of a heart attack in the hospital.

Now it is my heart that is aching. I have to hold on to the door. Everything around me is spinning. My head doesn't know what to think. My thoughts are flying from one side to the other side.

Mrs. Smith

My heart is feeling very heavy and wants to drop into my stomach. Why did Mrs. Smith go away without saying goodbye? The woman in the doorway asks me if I want to come in. I don't want to go into Mrs. Smith's apartment if she is not there. I shake my head and go back to my own apartment. It's Monday, ten minutes after 5:00 p.m. Every Monday at this time, I'm sitting in Mrs. Smith's living room, eating Oreos. Not today. Today Mrs. Smith died. I feel sick. My stomach aches. But it's not aching because I've been laughing too much. Without Mrs. Smith, I don't want to laugh.

QUESTIONS/THOUGHTS

- Have you ever lost someone close?
- What did it feel like?

Whenever I don't know what to do, when I don't have a solution for a problem, I call my staff person. His name is Peter. Peter says I can call him when there is an emergency. Today there is an emergency. Peter says I should cry. He says I will feel better afterward. I don't understand that. Why should I feel better after crying? If Mrs. Smith could come back I would feel better. Then I could play Parcheesi with her every Monday again. Peter says I have to accept that Mrs. Smith won't be coming back. I find that very hard. I want her to come back. That's why I don't want to accept that she won't come back. I try to cry a bit, because my heart is aching so much. That doesn't really help. Talking to Peter and listening to his voice helps me. I don't know what to do next Monday at 5:00 p.m. I ask Peter if he has an idea.

Peter says it's important that we find something I can do instead every Monday at 5:00 p.m. I don't want to find something else I can do. I want Mrs. Smith to be there again next Monday at 5:00 p.m. But she won't come back. I do understand this now.

QUESTIONS/THOUGHTS

- What does it feel like when a routine is interrupted?
- Who helps you when you are feeling down?
- What would you do if you were David?

I've been dreaming of Mrs. Smith. We were laughing at her jokes. And I was eating Oreos. We were playing Parcheesi and Mrs. Smith won. I was a little disappointed. When I woke up I remembered that Mrs. Smith was gone forever. That really hurt. I felt a bad pain in my heart.

What Do You Want on Your Pancakes?

It is Monday, 5:00 p.m. I ring Mrs. Smith's doorbell. No answer. I ring again. I want to know for sure that Mrs. Smith is gone and won't come back. She doesn't open the door. I go back to my own apartment. Now I know that she won't come back. Mrs. Smith will not be there on Mondays.

Now I hear my doorbell ringing. I don't know who it could be. I open the door, and in front of my door stands a woman. Somehow she looks familiar to me but I don't know where I know her from. "Hello, I'm Mrs. Smith's daughter. You came to visit her last week," says the woman in my doorway. Now I remember. She's the woman who answered Mrs. Smith's door last week. Now she is standing in my doorway. "My mother told me how much she looked forward to playing Parcheesi with you every Monday. When I was younger I played Parcheesi with her. Then I had to move away. I could not visit my mother very often after I moved away. I would like to give the game to you as a present. That will help you to remember my mother."

I think that is a good idea. I want to remember Mrs. Smith. Once I'm old I want to tell the others about our Mondays. The woman in the doorway tells me, "Tomorrow I have to go back home. But if you want to we could play Parcheesi together now. My name is Miss Smith. What is your name?"

"My name is David," I say.

FOR FUN ACTIVITIES RELATED TO OUR STORIES,
USE THE QR CODE PROVIDED.

If at First
You Don't Succeed

MY NAME IS TOM ADAMS. I am thirty years old and I have Down Syndrome. Up until six months ago I lived in a house with my parents. But I have goals, and one of them is to be more independent.

So six months ago I moved out of my parents' home and into a home with two other men who also have developmental or intellectual disabilities. So far, the move has been a success, and things have been going smoothly.

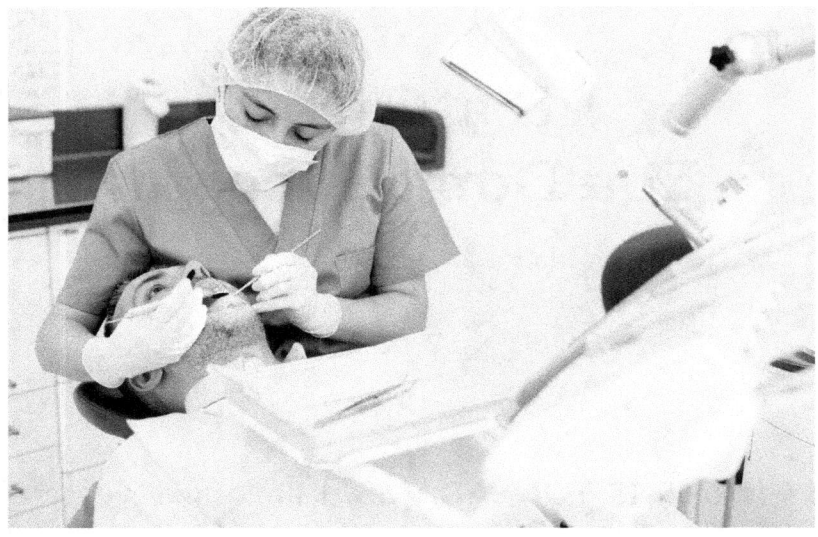

Last Tuesday when I went to the dentist for my regular checkup, Dr. Sweeney told me that one of my bottom wisdom teeth (the ones way in the back) had a broken root and had to be extracted. I asked what that meant. He said he had to pull it out. Ouch! That didn't sound good.

He said the sooner the better, so they made an appointment for Thursday.

I was scared. I've never had a tooth extracted before. and when I told my parents about it on the phone that night, they offered to take care of everything for me, but I said no. I wanted to be independent.

QUESTIONS/THOUGHTS

- Do you want to be more independent in your life?
- Do you like going to the dentist or not?
- Have you ever had a tooth pulled out?

Wednesday night before the extraction I was too nervous to get to sleep. I decided to watch my favorite movie of all time, *50 First Dates*. It's a romantic comedy starring Drew Barrymore and Adam Sandler. If you've never seen it, you should watch it! Without giving too much away, Drew Barrymore plays a young woman who was in a car accident and can't remember anything from one day to the next.

That includes Adam Sandler, who really likes her. So, because she can't remember HIM from one day to the next, they wind up having fifty first dates!

At the end of the movie, I was still too nervous to sleep. But the movie had gotten me thinking about all of the first dates I had been on. In the movie, Adam Sandler got to go out with Drew Barrymore for one first date after another. In my real life, all of my first dates had been disasters, some worse than others. Honestly, I was about ready to give up on the whole dating thing altogether.

If I told you about all of my disastrous first dates, it might give you nightmares. But I want you to understand why I have given up on dating, so I will share three of my dating experiences that were especially bad.

My very first date was with a girl named Helen. I was really excited about going out with her. I thought the two of us would walk over to the neighborhood Dairy Queen and get ice cream cones.

When she answered the door at her house, she came out with her FATHER and all three of us went to the Dairy Queen. I guess they never heard the expression, "Three's a crowd!"

Another first date I'd rather forget was when my mom fixed me up with Sonia, the daughter of one of her friends. We made plans to meet at a local diner. She told me she'd be wearing a bright yellow hoodie that I couldn't miss. I spotted Sonia sitting at the counter as soon as I entered the diner.

What Do You Want on Your Pancakes?

As I walked over to where she was sitting, she stood up. She had to be at least a foot taller than me! And if that wasn't bad enough, she laughed like a hyena! I mean, maybe she was just nervous like I was, but that laugh was enough to peel the wallpaper right off the wall!

But the absolute WORST date of all time, the date that convinced me to quit dating altogether, was with Catherine. She invited me over to her house to watch a movie. She greeted me at the door and invited me in. We sat down on the couch. So far, so good, right? Then I looked around. There were cats everywhere. Cats on the bookshelves. Cats on the refrigerator. On the counter. On the stove. On the dining room table. There must have been at least twenty of them!

The air was so strong with the stench of cats that my eyes started to water. I was having trouble breathing. I choked out the words, "I'm allergic to cats!" and bolted out the door, gasping for breath and reaching for my inhaler.

QUESTIONS/THOUGHTS

- Have you ever been out on a date? If so, was it fun?

- Tom is allergic to cats. Do you have any allergies? What are they?

So, fast forward to Thursday morning, the day of the extraction. I was sitting on the front porch of the group home where I live, waiting for my coworker Cheryl to pick me up and take me to the dentist's office for the procedure.

What Do You Want on Your Pancakes?

Cheryl and I both work at Publix, the local grocery store. I collect the carts in the parking lot and do other odd jobs. Cheryl has been stocking shelves for even longer than I have been collecting carts. Cheryl is about my height, with brown hair and hazel eyes. She laughs a lot, but not loudly. She has a dog named Jack, but she doesn't really care for cats. She is on the autism spectrum and had moved into her own apartment about the same time I moved into my group home, so we had a lot in common. She was working Tuesday afternoon after my dental checkup, and in the break room I had confided in her about having to have my wisdom tooth pulled out, how nervous I was, and how I wanted to be independent and do it without my parents' help.

"Hey, I can give you a ride to the dentist on Thursday. It's my day off," Cheryl had said.

Thursday morning I heard Cheryl's cherry-red Volkswagen bug before it rounded the corner of my street. She was saving up for a new muffler.

As I hopped into the passenger seat she said, "Gee, Tom, you look like you didn't sleep at all last night!"

"You got that right, Cheryl. I am a nervous wreck about getting this tooth pulled out. Maybe I SHOULD have asked my parents to take care of everything," I replied.

"Tom, you've got this! Look, if you want me to, I could come in with you for moral support," Cheryl suggested.

As we pulled into the parking lot at the dentist's office, I heaved a sigh of relief. "That would be great, Cheryl. I really appreciate it!"

"No problem, Tom. That's what friends are for," she said.

I don't remember too much of what happened at the dentist's office. I remember that Dr. Sweeney said it was okay for Cheryl to sit in the procedure room with me.

I remember grabbing her hand and squeezing it as they hooked up the intravenous to give me anesthesia to put me to sleep while they pulled out my tooth...

I was still gripping her hand when I woke up. It was over. I had done it! I remember Dr. Sweeney saying something about that wisdom tooth not causing me any more problems.

Cheryl and I walked out into the parking lot and hopped into her car. She put her hand on my shoulder. "Hey, Tom, I know this has been the world's weirdest date up until now, but how do you feel about stopping at the diner on the way home? I think a milkshake would taste great and probably feel good on your mouth right now too." She laughed.

I looked at Cheryl and smiled thoughtfully. Maybe giving up on dating altogether wasn't such a good idea. You know what they say, "If at first you don't succeed, try, try again!"

Questions/Thoughts

- What kind of car would you like to have?
- Do you think Tom and Cheryl will continue to be friends?
- Where do you think they might go on their next date?

**FOR FUN ACTIVITIES RELATED TO OUR STORIES,
USE THE QR CODE PROVIDED.**

The Baby Elephant

HAPPY BIRTHDAY

As the sun rose on Saturday morning, a sense of happy excitement hung over the Berlin Zoo in Germany. Why? Because last night something wonderful had happened. A new baby elephant had been born!

The night before had been very long and very tense. The entire herd of elephants shared a sense of anxiety. Sunita, the mother of the newborn elephant, had been pregnant for twenty-two months before she was finally ready to give birth. That is almost two years!

Shortly before Sunita went into labor, she chose a safe spot in the elephant park to have her baby. Because elephants give birth standing up and the baby comes out with its head and forelegs first, Sunita had to find a nice soft spot for the baby to land without hurting himself. Sunita's labor went on for more than a day, but she was not alone. All the other females from the herd stood by her and helped her through her labor pains.

The Baby Elephant

Grace and Joe were the caretakers of the elephant herd. Because they wanted to be sure to be close by when Sunita gave birth, they had been sleeping at the zoo every night for the past two weeks. Last night, while Sunita was in labor, they watched closely but from a distance, following the birth on video cameras. Grace and Joe wanted the birth to be as natural as possible, and were very relieved when the baby finally emerged from Sunita's belly. It was a boy! Everyone cheered and was happy that both Sunita and her new baby were fine.

So, as the zoo opened its doors this Saturday morning, at first it was like any other Saturday morning at the zoo. But as news of the new elephant baby spread on social media, TV, and local radio, more and more people headed to the elephant park to see the new baby elephant for themselves. At first there was only a single row of people standing at the edges of the elephant enclosure.

But by eleven o'clock visitors were already crowded around, hoping to catch a glimpse of the newborn elephant. As the size of the crowd around the elephant enclosure continued to grow, the mood of the visitors remained upbeat.

Everyone wanted to get a photo of Sunita and her baby. Lots of people held up their smartphones to capture a photo, but others had brought large cameras with long lenses to be able to zoom in better. Once the baby elephant delighted everyone in the crowd by stretching its little trunk in the air and making a soft *tooo* sound. The entire crowd burst into applause and hoped for another little *tooo*.

It takes human babies a long time to stand up and walk, but baby elephants can stand up right away. Walking was a bit of a challenge for the baby elephant because his little legs got wobbly, and he fell over. But Sunita, his mama, was there to help him back to his feet, reaching under her baby's belly with her trunk and standing him back up.

The Baby Elephant

The baby elephant was very small compared to his parents. Standing under his mother, his little trunk groped along her belly, searching for mother's milk. Sunita was very careful not to hurt the baby, since she was much larger and much heavier than he was.

Questions/Thoughts

- What is your favorite animal and why?
- What do you think it would be like to be a zoo caretaker?
- Have you ever been to a zoo or an animal park?

THE ELEPHANT FAMILY

While the baby elephant nursed, Sunita, his mother, stood very still. She munched on hay and carrots and was not disturbed by the other elephants, who seemed to know she was busy doing an important job. A baby elephant drinks up to ten liters of milk every day.

Shiva was the father of the little one. He chased away the other elephants of the herd when they came too close to the baby. He pushed them aside with his trunk, and sometimes he raised his trunk and trumpeted loudly. He wanted everyone to know that he was a proud father.

In addition to his parents, the baby elephant had lots of "aunts" in the herd to help care for him and make sure he grew and developed well.

There was one thing that the baby elephant did not yet have, though, and that was a suitable name! The elephant caretakers, Grace and Joe, thought that because Sunita and Shiva were Indian elephants, their son should have an Indian name.

The Baby Elephant

Grace and Joe decided to let all visitors to the elephant park at the Berlin Zoo have a chance to suggest a name for the new addition to the zoo. Every day more and more visitors came to see the baby elephant and take his picture. Many of them left suggestions for what to name the baby, but he didn't seem to care. He was just happy to be with his herd, drink mother's milk, and sleep.

THE NAME CONTEST

Today was the last day of the name contest for the new baby elephant. Each suggestion had been dropped into a large box at the entrance to the elephant park. The box was filled almost to the top with little slips of paper. Some suggestions were thoughtfully written with great care and with almost perfect handwriting, while others were awkwardly scrawled by young children. Grace and Joe, the elephant caretakers, were excited to read them all!

They started unrolling the pieces of paper. Many of the children had put a lot of effort into writing their notes. Grace opened a folded piece of paper and found a drawing of the new baby elephant. Under the painted picture it said: *I would like the new baby elephant to be called "Amal." Amal means "hope." I hope that the baby elephant will have a nice life with his herd here in the zoo.* Grace decided to put this sweet note in the heart-shaped box that she and Joe were using to sort out the best name suggestions.

Grace unfolded some more slips of paper. *Jadoo*, *Himal*, and *Bodhi*. None of these names appealed to Grace, so none of them made it into the heart-shaped box.

It was Joe's turn to unfold a suggestion. On the paper, in beautifully written script, it said *Arunja*. Joe thought about whether the name fit the baby elephant. He read the name aloud. "Arunja, Arunja." He liked the name, and put it in the heart-shaped box. The next suggestion was *Rajiv*.

Joe looked over at the baby elephant and decided he didn't look like a Rajiv, and so that slip of paper didn't make it to the heart-shaped box.

The job of going through all these suggestions took longer than Grace and Joe had expected. Finally, Grace pulled the last suggestion out of the box. She unfolded it to see a sketch of a Hindu god with an elephant head and four arms. Under the sketch, in red letters, was the name *Ganesha*.

Underneath was the explanation that Ganesha is one of the most important gods in India, worshipped in almost every street shrine. Ganesha is the son of Shiva and Parvati. Grace looked closely at the image of the god. She liked the friendly expression on his face. She also was taken with the connection to the Hindu story, since the baby elephant's father was also named Shiva. She decided that this suggestion was a good one and put it in the heart-shaped box.

Questions/Thoughts

- Which of the suggested names do you like best?
- Ask your seatmate or someone who is around you which name he or she likes best.
- Work with a partner to think of another Indian name for a baby elephant.
- Make a prediction of which name is going to win the contest.

The Baby Elephant

Joe and Grace had one more job to do, the difficult task of choosing a winning name from the slips of paper in the heart-shaped box. They read each name aloud to each other again. They liked the sound of all the names. They tried and tried, but they couldn't choose one name. Just as they were about to give up, one of their coworkers, Sonja, entered their office. Grace and Joe showed her the remaining slips of paper and asked for her opinion. Sonja took her time, looking closely at each suggestion in the heart-shaped box.

After ten minutes, she had made up her mind. "Since the father of the new baby elephant is named Shiva, we should name the baby Ganesha. It was meant to be. Also, the elephant-shaped head of this god is perfect!" Joe and Grace had to agree with her. The contest had a winner, and their baby elephant finally had a name: Ganesha!

THE OTHER LITTLE ELEPHANT

But Ganesha wasn't the only little elephant in the elephant park at the Berlin Zoo. Just two weeks ago another little elephant named Bina was the center of attention when she celebrated her first birthday. Many visitors came to the zoo that day especially for her birthday. All over the zoo, children were seen pulling their parents in the direction of the elephant enclosure.

Children shouted, "Dad, come quickly! I want to wish Bina a happy birthday!" Many visitors wrote cards or drew pictures for her birthday.

Bina, of course, could not read the cards. But she did love all the attention.

Whenever Bina splashed water on her back with her trunk, the birthday guests laughed and cheered. They were thrilled to watch Bina play, and stayed to watch her for a long time. Bina was happy about her visitors. But now the visitors all crowded around the new baby, Ganesha. They spent their time watching him and laughing when he tripped over his own wobbly little legs.

JEALOUSY

Bina was jealous. Just two weeks ago on her birthday, she was the center of attention. Now the visitors came just to look at the new baby elephant, Ganesha. No one was interested in her anymore! Bina was bored. She wanted to play with the new baby elephant, but whenever she got close, the baby's father pushed her aside with his trunk. Bina almost lost her balance and fell, but she was old enough to catch herself before she did. She didn't give up and tried again. This time, Bina snuck up behind Ganesha. But Shiva, the baby's dad, noticed her and chased her away. Still, Bina did not give up. She tried to get to the baby Ganesha from the other side. But the father was faster. He again blocked Bina's way with his trunk. Sadly, Bina trotted away defeated, at least for the moment.

Bina went outside to join the rest of the herd. She found the ball that the caretakers, Joe and Grace, had made for her. It was hollow on the inside, and they stuffed it with carrots, so when Bina bounced it against the wall, a few of the carrots fell out, and she could have a treat. This usually kept Bina occupied for hours, but today she played with it for a few minutes. When she looked up, she saw no visitors watching her and laughing at her antics. Not a single one. They were all in the elephant house watching the new baby elephant, Ganesha.

TOGETHER AT LAST

Bina trotted back inside. Sunita and the baby elephant Ganesha were standing alone in the corner. Shiva, the father, had gone to the water basin, where he was drinking and splashing himself with water. Bina decided to take advantage of the situation and ran a little faster. She was close enough now to reach out with her trunk and touch the baby elephant.

Surprised, Ganesha turned around so quickly that he almost lost his balance and fell. But he caught himself, staying safely on his feet, and used his own trunk to reach out in Bina's direction. His trunk was much thinner and shorter than hers, but they touched trunks in a kind of elephant handshake and greeted each other.

Shiva, the baby's father, was finished at the water basin and turned around to see the two small elephants. At first, he reached out to bat Bina away. But then he saw the two young elephants were playing. His Ganesha had made a friend!

Now Shiva no longer chases Bina away. Instead, he watches over both elephants. Bina has stopped digging and watches Ganesha excitedly. Bina is happy that they have developed a game together and that she no longer has to play alone. As she looks around, Bina realizes that there is a crowd of visitors who are not just watching Ganesha, the new baby elephant.

No. They are watching the two little elephants, Ganesha and Bina, and laughing at them and taking pictures with their smartphones. How nice, thinks Bina, that a new baby elephant has been born into the herd.

QUESTIONS/THOUGHTS

- Have you ever been jealous of someone else?
- Do you have siblings or friends who have made you jealous?
- Do you have a special friend you like to spend time with?

FOR FUN ACTIVITIES RELATED TO OUR STORIES, USE THE QR CODE PROVIDED.

Captain Walt Thomas

MY NAME IS WALT THOMAS. I am a retired airline pilot. My wife, Sandy, and I live in Denver, Colorado. Flying airplanes was a cool job because it gave me a chance to see a lot of interesting places. I also met several well-known people, like Taylor Swift and former President Obama. I had to retire because of my age. If it had been up to me, I probably would have worked a few more years. Most of my time now is spent playing golf and fixing things around the house. Sandy still works as a lawyer.

What Do You Want on Your Pancakes?

We never had children. Our dogs, Hector and Lopez, are like our children and keep us busy. They are both pugs. People usually look at us funny when we tell them their names.

Things have been different since I retired. I have more time on my hands. You can only play so much golf and fix so many things at home. I was used to staying busy. Sandy keeps telling me I should volunteer somewhere. She says, "Walt, you have so much to offer. You are friendly and very kind. You are also funny, big guy. I know there is a place somewhere that would love to have you volunteer." I know that she is right. I need to find a place where I can help and feel useful.

One day I was playing golf with two other retired pilot buddies, Ron Tingle and Omar Luck. We had all put in at least thirty years flying for United Airlines. None of us were very good at golf. Ron liked to play. Omar and I played mostly to have something to do.

We all liked to share stories about flying and to have lunch after we played. I told the guys I was thinking about doing volunteer work. Omar was interested. He had already been thinking about volunteering at the animal shelter. Ron still worked part time at his brother's pest control company called Don't Pester Me! Ron did not think he had time to volunteer.

QUESTIONS/THOUGHTS

- Do you know anyone who is retired?
- Have you done any volunteer work?
- What would it be like to be an airline pilot?

Later that day, I was outside at the house. Sandy had asked me to fix the garage door opener. She was at work. Out of the blue, I started feeling dizzy and then fell to the ground. I tried to stand up but could not. I was having pain in my chest. The only thing I could think to do was to shout HELP!

After two or three shouts, our neighbor Beth Ann came over and knew right away I needed medical attention. "I think we need to call 911 and get you to the hospital, Walt. Is that okay with you?" she asked. I agreed. Beth Ann also said she was going to call Sandy.

The emergency room was busy. There were a lot of people around me trying to find out what was wrong. Everyone was very nice. They told me that my wife was in the waiting room and that they would bring her back as soon as possible.

One of the nurses, Mark, said, "You are doing great, Captain Thomas. Try to relax. We should be done poking you in a few minutes, and then we are going to send you for x-rays."

I understood what Mark was saying but was plenty worried. I was able to say, "Thanks, everyone," but that was about it.

What Do You Want on Your Pancakes?

After x-rays, Mark brought Sandy back to see me. Boy, was I happy to see her. I could tell Sandy was worried even though she tried to act calm. A few minutes later, Dr. Milton and some other younger doctors came in. They said I had had a mild heart attack. They wanted to admit me to the hospital for more testing. Sandy had a bunch of questions. What caused it? Will he need surgery? How long will he need to be in the hospital?

Dr. Milton said, "These are all great questions. We will try to have answers for you as fast as we can. You both will be seeing a lot of us once you get upstairs. Very nice to have met you, Captain and Ms. Thomas. My team and I will be taking care of you in the hospital." Dr. Milton smiled and waved goodbye.

Intensive care is where patients are watched very closely. My nurse, Alice Frank, only took care of me and one other patient. Alice told me how much she respected Dr. Milton. "That lady is one fine doctor, Captain Thomas!" she said.

Alice and I became friends pretty much from the moment we met. She was funny, friendly, and very kind. She made sure I was comfortable and explained everything she did for me and why she did it. My other nurse, when Alice left, was Todd. He had recently graduated from nursing school and was very serious. He took wonderful care of me but was not as warm and fuzzy as Alice.

QUESTIONS/THOUGHTS

- Have you ever been in an emergency room? If so, what was it like?
- Do you know anyone who is funny, friendly, and very kind?
- What has been your experience with doctors?

Three days later it was time for me to come home. I could not wait to be in my own bed with my own pillow. Everyone in the hospital was very friendly. I could not have asked for better care.

But I was happy to leave. Dr. Milton would still be my cardiologist (heart doctor). Her office was close to my house. I would be going there three times a week for cardiac rehab, where you do exercises and gain strength. They also teach you how to eat the right food and other ways to take care of your body. Right then, I wanted to do everything I was told to get better as soon as possible.

A few days later Sandy and I had a heart-to-heart talk. She wanted me to know how worried she was. "I really want you to work hard in rehab and do everything they tell you, Walt," she said. I could tell she meant business. Sandy is the love of my life, and I would do anything for her. As we were talking, our pugs, Hector and Lopez, came over. It was like they knew something was going on.

Sandy and I looked at one another and smiled. I hugged Sandy and told her everything was going to be okay. Then we took the two boys out for a long walk.

Finally, it came to me. Out of the blue. I knew what kind of volunteer work I wanted to do and where I wanted to do it. First things first, however, I needed to finish rehab. There were ten of us in my rehab group. All different ages and from all walks of life. Some of us were retired. There was a stay-at-home dad and four people with paid jobs. Some of us were in better shape than others.

Our instructor, Gail Gibbson, a physical therapist, explained what we would be doing for the next several weeks. "First, I want to welcome you. You all have some type of heart condition. We are here to help you learn how to better take care of yourselves. We will be doing a lot of walking and other exercises to help you get stronger. Each of you will have your own individual plan. My staff and I will guide and support you. I also hope you will support and encourage each other."

That night, Sandy got home after me. When she walked into the kitchen, I could tell something was wrong. "What is going on, Sandy?" I asked.

"I was in a car accident on my way home. I had to stop for a red light, then BANG, a car hit me from behind. We are lucky that there was not much damage to my car. The police came and made a report. They also made sure that both cars were drivable. I feel okay except for a small headache and some neck pain.

"The other driver was a teenager, and I felt bad for her because she had just gotten her driver's license. Anyhow, can we order a pizza and go to bed early?" she asked.

Later that night, Sandy had trouble sleeping. Her headache was worse, and she could barely move her head. I told her we needed to go to the emergency room. She did not want to go. I said, "We need to make sure that there is not something seriously wrong. Please do this for me."

It did not take long for us to get to the hospital ER. The waiting room was empty. It only took a few minutes for them to see Sandy.

And guess who her nurse was? It was Mark, the same nurse I had a few weeks ago. We were very happy to see one another. They took x-rays and found out Sandy had a mild concussion and a serious case of whiplash, all caused by the car accident.

What Do You Want on Your Pancakes?

After three hours at the hospital, they sent Sandy home in a neck brace and gave her medication to help with her headache. We were happy to be home. Lopez and Hector were so happy to see us they would have done back flips if they could have. We were both tired but not sleepy. We talked about how lucky we were to have each other.

I said, "The hospital has also been great to us. I decided the other day at rehab I want to start volunteering there once we are both fully healthy again."

Sandy was very happy for me. She then said, even with a weak voice, "Maybe I will start working part time and do some volunteering at the hospital myself."

The dogs looked at us like they were saying, "What about us?"

I met some great people at rehab. There were four of us that really got along well. Gus was the stay-at-home dad with twin girls, April and May. Ida, a bookkeeper, was a single mom of two teenage boys named Arnold and Gill. And lastly there was the leader of our gang, Bob Jackson, whom we always called Big Bobby. He was a retired Baptist minister. While we did not have a lot in common, we all just clicked from the very beginning. We gave a lot of high fives and did not mind making fun of ourselves. We were very positive, glass-half-full kind of people.

The gang called me Captain. We made plans to hang out together after rehab. They all asked me to fly them to Casper, Wyoming, for a day trip. Casper has a wonderful park with a great big waterfall. There is also a wonderful breakfast and lunch restaurant called Eggington's. I told them my golf buddy Ron Tingle owned a single-engine plane that he might let me borrow. We could all pitch in for the gas. The group was pumped!

QUESTIONS/THOUGHTS

- Do you have a group of friends you hang out with? What kinds of things do you do together?
- What is your favorite restaurant and why?
- What would it be like to fly in a small airplane?
- Does your pet know when you are feeling happy or sad?

I began volunteering at the hospital about a month after rehab. First, I was interviewed about what made me interested in volunteering and the types of things I might be interested in doing. Then they checked to see if I had a criminal record and made sure my vaccinations were up to date. The staff in the volunteer office could not have been nicer. They needed someone to take flowers up to patients' rooms and greet people as they came into the hospital. Their need was a great match with what I wanted to do.

I signed up to volunteer on Thursdays from 10:00 to 2:00. I really enjoy helping. I might sign up for another day of the week, but I'm not sure yet. What I like most is spending time with the patients after taking flowers and sometimes even balloons to their rooms. It is great to see them smile when I walk in. Then they get even more excited after finding out who the gift is from.

What Do You Want on Your Pancakes?

One day I got to meet a young man named Hank. He had been in the hospital a few days because he had fluid in his lungs. The flowers I brought were from his friends at Learning Never Ends, a day program for people with intellectual disabilities. Just like my friends at rehab, I hit it off with Hank right away. We talked for a long time. I could not understand everything he said, but it did not matter.

As I was about to leave, Hank asked if I would come back to see him.

I said, "How about tomorrow?"

Hank said, "Sure thing! I can't wait."

I made sure it would be okay to visit Hank even if I was not on duty as a volunteer. The volunteer office said it would be fine.

The next morning, I told my golf buddies about starting to volunteer at the hospital. Ron asked me how I liked it. "It has been great," I said. Then I told him about Hank. He seemed interested.

"Please keep me posted about how you are enjoying it. Who knows, maybe I will be interested in helping there at some point. I'm not as busy as I thought I was going to be with the exterminating business," he admitted. Ron told me that he was fine with me borrowing his airplane and that he would cover the gas cost.

"Thanks Ron, you are a real pal!" I said.

He put his arm over my shoulder and replied, "I am just happy you made such a great recovery in rehab. Omar and I would be lost without you on the golf course."

That afternoon, Hank had great news for me. He had been cleared to go back to the house he shared with two other men. "Do you think we can still be friends after I leave the hospital? I would really like you to meet my roommates, Mark and Ed. I know they would like to meet you too," he said.

We shared our phone numbers, and he promised to call soon. I asked if he needed a ride home, but he said a staff member from his home was picking him up. I did not know where Hank was from or anything about his disability. It did not matter to me. What I did know was that we both liked dogs, country western music, and hot fudge sundaes.

Over the next few months, Hank and I hung out about once a week. Turns out he had been in the hospital for complications from a long-term heart condition. We would do things like go to the movies, take walks with Hector and Lopez, and listen to country-western music at each other's houses. We even helped each other out in our gardens. Hank and I just clicked together. I got to know his roommates, Mark and Ed, and found out more about his family. Sandy and I had a few friends who thought that we were being nice to Hank because of his disability.

That wasn't true, and we did not stay friends with them very long. I never looked at it like I was helping Hank out. We were just friends, plain and simple.

QUESTIONS/THOUGHTS

- What makes a good friend?
- Would you like to meet Captain Thomas and Hank, and if so, why?
- If you were writing this story, how would you finish it? What would happen next?
  Or, did it end just fine?

FOR FUN ACTIVITIES RELATED TO OUR STORIES,
USE THE QR CODE PROVIDED.

Muffin World

<u>NARRATOR:</u> *Hello! My name is Rudy Santino. I used to own a small bakery in Iron Mountain, Michigan. That is a thing of the past. I retired about two years ago and sold the business to my daughter, Rose. She decided to change the name of my bakery from Rudy's to Muffin World. What follows is a play about Muffin World. I will be your narrator. Get ready to meet some interesting people and experience exciting twists and turns. Yes, there will be a few surprises, so hold on to your hats and socks if you are wearing them. Now let me introduce you to the characters.*

ROSE: The hardworking, thirty-four-year-old owner of Muffin World. Rose is my daughter and quick to speak her mind. She also helps other people whenever she can. Rose loves cats and drives a Ford F-150 pickup truck.

ARMANDO (ARNIE): The thirty-eight-year-old lead baker at Muffin World and on-again, off-again boyfriend of Rose. He moved to Iron Mountain to take care of his sick father, who has since passed away. Arnie has a temper and can be moody. He also tends to be a know-it-all. However, he works hard and can be kindhearted. Arnie has a dog named Gus, who is a boxer. Arnie loves to snowboard.

ROCCO: My twenty-four-year-old nephew and Rose's cousin. He works part time at Muffin World helping Arnie in the kitchen. He also works part time collecting tickets and selling popcorn at the local movie theater.

Rocco lives with his parents, loves playing video games, and enjoys collecting baseball cards. Rocco would like to have a girlfriend.

DEE: A sixty-five-year-old regular customer at Muffin World. She recently retired as director of the town library. Dee was born in Iron Mountain. She has never married, has four cats, and knows practically everyone in town. She is outgoing, well-liked, and has a wonderful smile. There are many times, however, when Dee feels lonely.

JOANIE: A nineteen-year-old high school student who uses a wheelchair. She is doing job training at Muffin World. She helps to package muffins and clean the small eating area that has five tables. Joanie is shy and lacks self-confidence. She lives with her mother, who owns a plumbing company.

LOCKHART: Joanie's fifty-nine-year-old job coach. He helps her learn work skills and how to act on the job. He is an all-around nice guy, who drove a truck for a living after twenty five years of serving in the Navy. He likes to help people learn work skills so they can find meaningful jobs. He is a coach for the high school boy's hockey team. He has been divorced twice and has no children. He loves collecting antiques.

SHERIFF BETH WAGNOR: Chief of the Dickinson County Sheriff's Department. No one knows her age except for her husband, Corbin. Beth and Corbin have two children named Jack and Jill. They breed poodles five miles out of town.

BETTY SUE: A thirty-six-year-old country western singer who is Rose's best friend. Betty Sue has yet to find the man of her dreams. Rose thinks Betty Sue is too picky. She helps at the counter at Muffin World when she can.

Rose and Betty Sue talk at least once a day. Her dream is to someday appear at the Grand Ole Opry.

ACT I - SCENE 1

NARRATOR: _Rose and Arnie are on their way to work at Muffin World. It is 4:30 in the morning. For the past four months, they have been getting along well together. When their relationship is good, they live together at Arnie's. When they are not getting along, they stay in their own homes. I do not fully understand their relationship. All I can say is, when it works it works, and when it doesn't it doesn't._

ROSE: Man, is it early. Tell me again why you need help this morning.

ARNIE: We have a big order of muffins that are being picked up at 7:00 am. And by the way, they would have ordered donuts, too, if we made them.

ROSE: Let's not have this discussion now. You know that muffins are what we specialize in and what we are known for.

ARNIE: Okay, okay. I just think we could make more money if there was a larger selection of bakery items to choose from.

ROSE: I hear you, Arnie. You sound like my father. Maybe we do need to make different types of bakery items. It is just that I have so much going on right now and don't need another thing to deal with.

ARNIE: I am sorry, Rose. I did not know you had that much going on. Is there something I can help you with?

ROSE: That is sweet of you, Arnie. It is just that I need to have some dental work done, and I am worried about how much it will cost. My water heater at home needs to be fixed or replaced. I also need to have a talk with Rocco about getting to work on time. I also heard that he has been flirting with the young women who come into Muffin World. Should I go on?

ARNIE: No, no, I get it. I know you get upset when I lose my temper and act like I know everything. I will try harder, I promise.

ROSE: Thank you, Arnie, that means a lot.

SCENE 2

NARRATOR: *Rocco arrives at 7:15, fifteen minutes late to work. Dee is already enjoying her usual cup of black coffee and banana nut muffin while seated at the counter.*

DEE: Late again, Rocco? You might want to get a new alarm clock.

ROCCO: I know, it really isn't my alarm clock's fault.

DEE: Maybe you should think about going to bed earlier. But listen, I am not your boss.

What Do You Want on Your Pancakes?

NARRATOR: _Rose steps out from the kitchen just as Dee is telling Rocco she is not his boss. Rose tries to keep her cool, but she is not happy. She tells Rocco to get ready for work. Then Rose asks him to stop by her office in fifteen minutes. Rocco reports to her office on time._

ROSE: Hi, Rocco, please have a seat. Do you like your job here at Muffin World?

ROCCO: I love my job here. I would not mind working here full time. Why do you ask?

ROSE: Because you come in late. Our customers notice it too. I have enough to worry about without you coming to work late. Things must change or I am going to fire you. You also have been flirting with young women who come into the shop. This must stop immediately.

ROCCO: Gee, I did not know how bad things were.

ROSE: Right, there is the problem. You are twenty four years old, Rocco, and should know not to be late or overly friendly with female customers.

<u>NARRATOR</u>: *Rocco begins to cry. Rose hands him a tissue.*

<u>ROCCO</u>: I hear what you are saying, Rose. I am so sorry to have let you down. You do have every right to fire me. If you give me a second chance, I promise to change things around.

<u>ROSE</u>: Let's give it two weeks and see how things go.

<u>NARRATOR</u>: *Rocco thanks Rose, and he shakes her hand. He then returns to the kitchen. It was clear that Rose meant business. Rocco starts to think about ways he could stop being late and being overly friendly with customers.*

- *Get a louder alarm clock.*
- *Go to sleep earlier.*
- *Have a friend call to remind him.*
- *Remind himself about how important his job is to him.*
- *Think about how he doesn't want to let Rose down.*

- *Put signs around his apartment saying* Grow Up, Be Responsible, *and* Don't Flirt.
- *Ask Rose to describe what flirting means and how he is flirting.*

SCENE 3

NARRATOR: *Dee is still hanging out at the counter and chatting with Sheriff Beth. Betty Sue is working behind the counter, having arrived at 8:00 a.m. sharp.*

DEE (in a soft voice)**:** You guys missed Rocco getting chewed out by Rose for being late. She was not a happy camper.

SHERIFF BETH: Well, I hope he learns his lesson. Sometimes a good chewing out can help turn things around. Sometimes not.

BETTY SUE: Rocco is a good kid. He just needs to grow up. Look at me, I am still growing up. And forget about asking, because I am not going to tell you my age.

DEE: I had people working for me at the library who needed a talking to. And then there were those that I had to fire. It was never easy. I had to keep reminding myself that what I was doing was best for the library.

SHERIFF BETH: I try to support the people who work for me. I try to be fair. At the end of the day, it is all about how well someone is doing their job. I also must deal with complaints about my police officers. Sometimes, I feel like a detective trying to decide who to believe. Being a boss is not easy.

NARRATOR: Sheriff Beth and Dee keep talking about what it is like to be a boss. They come up with a list: "What Makes a Good Employee."

DEE: Okay, Beth, here's the list we came up with. I titled it "What Makes a Good Employee."

- Gets to work on time.
- Works well with others.
- Knows when to ask for help and be open to feedback.
- Tries to improve skills and speed of work.

NARRATOR: *As they are talking, Rose walks in. She overhears part of what they have been talking about.*

ROSE: Maybe the two of you could teach me a thing or two about how to be a better boss.

DEE: From what I see you run a smooth business here.

SHERIFF BETH: I agree. You seem to relate well with your employees.

BETTY SUE: We think the world of you, Rose. But we also know that you will let us know if we do not do our jobs the right way. As for me, I know you have my best interests at heart, not only as a friend but also as an employee.

ROSE: You guys are making me blush. I really thank you for the kind things you have shared. Sometimes I get down on myself. I also want my dad to be proud of me. Don't forget, Rudy was not pleased that I changed the name of the bakery to Muffin World. And of course, Arnie and I do not always agree about the direction Muffin World is taking.

He wants us to slowly start serving a bigger variety of bakery items in addition to just muffins. So, stress is my middle name most days.

DEE: I hope you know we are all behind you, Rose. Anything we can do to help, just say the word.

SHERIFF BETH: We live in a small town where neighbors pull together. Anything you need Rose, just let us know.

SCENE 4

NARRATOR: *High school student Joanie and her job coach, Lockhart, enter the break room at Muffin World. Arnie, the baker, and Rocco, Rose's nephew, are already there. Everyone is talking about how much snow has already fallen and how much more is coming overnight. Iron Mountain gets tons of snow every year. Weather is a common topic of conversation.*

JOANIE: With this miserable weather, I felt like calling in sick for work today. Hopefully, someday I will be able to leave Iron Mountain and all this SNOW!

LOCKHART: I am proud of you for not calling in sick, Joanie. You have been doing so well with your job here at Muffin World.

ROCCO: I am proud of you too. It is important to take work seriously. I got into trouble this morning for being late to work. It really made me think how important my job is. And about the snow, I agree. It can be a royal pain.

ARNIE: I like the snow. It would be hard to snowboard without it. And I love to snowboard.

JOANIE: It is not just the snow but also the cold that I do not like. BRRRR!

ARNIE: Maybe you and Rocco can come snowboarding with me sometime. It is a blast, and I'd love to teach you guys how to do it.

ROCCO: That works for me. Thanks for offering, Arnie.

JOANIE: Nobody has offered to teach me how to do winter sports. Guess maybe they thought it would be too difficult since I use a wheelchair. Do you think there might be a way for me to snowboard even though I can't walk?

ARNIE: My father always used to tell me, "Where there is a will, there is a way." What he meant was, if you want something bad enough there is usually a way to get it. I will investigate what has been done for others who cannot use their legs, and we will go from there.

JOANIE: That makes sense to me. I am willing. Sign me up.

ROCCO: Count me in too.

LOCKHART: If you do not mind an old fart joining you, I would also like to give it a try.

ARNIE: Sounds like I have the makings of a class. This is very exciting. I will check with the ski hill and find out what times are available. You folks are my heroes for wanting to learn something new. I promise to make it fun. You will be snowboarding in no time.

NARRATOR: *Rose and Arnie are driving back to his house after work. They seem happy together.*

ROSE: It has been a busy day. First, I had to get up early. Then I had to talk to Rocco about being late to work and flirting with customers. I told him his job was on the line. I gave him two weeks to improve. I have a hunch that he will start doing better. The good news is that my dad found an almost new hot water heater for me. And a friend of his has offered to install it for free.

I also heard my dental work won't cost as much as I thought. It has turned into a not-so-bad day.

ARNIE: I'm happy for you. You deserve the best. My day was pretty good too. I have three people that want to learn how to snowboard. It will be fun to teach them.

ROSE: Lockhart and Joanie told me all about it. They were very excited. I'm happy for you, Arnie. Maybe we should order a pizza and open a bottle of wine to celebrate the great day we have had.

ARNIE: Sounds like a wonderful plan. You're the best.

QUESTIONS/THOUGHTS

- What do you do when you are having a bad day?
- Would you like to learn how to snowboard?
- How do you feel about cold weather and snow?
- How would you like to be treated by your boss?

ACT II - SCENE 1

NARRATOR: *Two weeks later, Lockhart, the job coach, and Joanie, a high school student, are meeting in the small classroom.*

LOCKHART: How is your day going, Joanie?

JOANIE: It has been okay. I have a lot of trouble with math, so I do not like that class. I am not crazy about my teacher, either. She always thinks I am not trying hard enough. Also, none of the desks in her classroom work for me, because I cannot get my wheelchair underneath them. It is a mess.

LOCKHART: Anything I can do to help?

JOANIE: I must take math. Because I am a senior in high school this year, math is a required course, so I will just have to grin and bear it.

LOCKHART: I know you are shy, and it's hard to speak up for yourself. But now might be a time to start speaking your mind. It will be good practice for the future at work and in your personal life.

JOANIE: Just thinking about that makes me nervous.

LOCKHART: I know it can be scary. Maybe I can help.

JOANIE: How would you do that?

LOCKHART: I could go with you to have a meeting with your teacher. You would then have support to help you to express your concerns.

JOANIE: I am not sure about talking to my teacher. She seems pretty set in her ways. I am afraid she will not be willing to change. You think it would be okay if my mother joined us as well? I think with you and mom there, I would feel more comfortable speaking up for myself.

LOCKHART: I think that is a great idea. Before the meeting, we can practice what you want to say. Sound like a plan?

JOANIE: Yes, it does. But I am still very nervous about doing it.

LOCKHART: Practicing what you will say will help.

SCENE 2

NARRATOR: _Back in the employee break room at Muffin World, about a week later. Rose had asked all the staff to join her for a meeting. She had also invited Dee, the former library director. I (Rudy) got a call from Rose a few days before, asking me to attend. She would not tell me what the meeting was about. I love my daughter and support her as much as I can. So, I did not push her for an answer about the reason for the meeting._

ROSE: Hi, everyone. I guess you are wondering why I called this meeting.

QUESTIONS/THOUGHTS

- Why do you think Rose called the meeting?
- Any idea why she invited her father and Dee?
- How do you feel about being kept in the dark, not knowing what a meeting is going to be about ahead of time?

ARNIE: No kidding. I don't think any of us have any idea of what you are thinking.

RUDY: I sure don't, and I'm your father.

DEE: Other than because I am an amazing person, I'm not sure why I am invited.

BETTY SUE: Here I am, your best friend, and I do not have a clue.

ROSE: Easy does it, everyone. You are here because I want to share some ideas with you. So just listen and try not to ask any questions until I am finished, even though it will be hard.

I am thinking about turning Muffin World into a Mexican restaurant and calling it La Rosita's. Don't worry, I am just kidding. But I do think it is time to make some changes around here. I would really like my dad to come back and join me in the business. He has so much to offer. I think we need to change the name of this place to Rose & Rudy's Bakery Delights. We can start making all sorts of delicious goodies.

Along with Dad, I am going to need help from everyone here to change and grow our business. Dee, you are here every day. I wonder if you could work at the counter a few days a week and help me come up with a business plan. Joanie, I would like to hire you when you finish high school this year. We all love you around here. Your social media skills could help us expand the business. Rocco, I think you would make a great full-time baker's assistant and could learn a lot from Arnie and Dad. Betty Sue, maybe you could help me pretty up this place and reach out to restaurants and grocery stores that might be willing to sell our baked goods. Arnie, I know you will do an amazing job putting together our new line of bakery items. With more help, you might be able to spend more time enjoying the ski hills and give me snowboard lessons. Lastly, maybe we could hire you, Lockhart, to do deliveries for us.

OK, that's it. I'm done. So what do you all think of my ideas? Do you have any questions or suggestions?

<u>NARRATOR</u>: *Of course, everyone had questions. I could not believe my ears. I was so proud of Rose. She can be set in her ways, and change is not easy for her. I was excited about helping at the bakery and loved the new name Rose came up with. I know there are lots of questions to be answered. I will do everything in my power to lend my support. Some of the questions that were asked:*

- *When will this new plan start?*
- *Are you really open to suggestions?*
- *It sounds like you want to grow the business a lot. Will that mean finding a new location?*
- *When did you decide this?*
- *Are we the only people who know?*
- *Can we tell other people?*

<u>RUDY</u>: These are all good questions, my friends. I think for now it might be a good idea for us just to relax and give the ideas some thought. That is what I plan to do. Also, maybe we should not talk to other people about this just yet. What do you all think?

ARNIE: I agree.

DEE: Me too.

ROCCO: I think it all sounds very exciting.

JOANIE: I agree with Rocco.

LOCKHART: I thought I was done driving a truck, but it might be fun to hit the road again. I really like all you guys and am very excited about the plan Rose presented.

ROSE: Thanks, everyone. Please come and see me over the next few weeks. Change is not easy, but together I think we can make this happen.

SCENE 3

NARRATOR: *Arnie is at home with Rose. They are getting ready for bed and talking at the same time.*

ARNIE: You did a great job today, Rose. Everyone was very surprised. I think it was a good idea to tell us all at once.

ROSE: I hope you are not mad at me for not telling you before I told the others.

ARNIE: To be honest with you, I was a little upset. But I now see the point of not telling me. You needed to think through the plan alone, and I respect that.

ROSE: You are right. This is something I needed to do on my own. I hope you know that I usually do not keep secrets from you.

ARNIE: Speaking of secrets, I have one or two of my own. I think the time to share the secrets would be tomorrow night over dinner.

ROSE: I can't wait that long. It will drive me nuts.

ARNIE: Okay, okay. I will tell you one secret now, then the other tomorrow night over dinner at our favorite restaurant, Happy Times. I am just going to tell you, then we need to get some rest. You can only ask two questions. I have been seeing a counselor for a few months to work on my temper and not act like a know-it-all. I think it has been helping, and I am hoping you have noticed a difference.

ROSE: That is wonderful, Arnie. I have noticed a difference. Thanks for sharing.

Sure, I have questions, but they can wait until tomorrow. I love you, and let's get some sleep.

QUESTIONS/THOUGHTS

- Is it okay to have secrets?
- What secret do you think Arnie is going to share with Rose tomorrow night?
- How do you feel about Muffin World changing to Rose and Rudy's Bakery Delights?
- What would be the first new bakery item you would add to the menu?

SCENE 4

NARRATOR: *Rose and Arnie arrive at Happy Times for dinner. Arnie had called ahead to request a quiet, out-of-the-way table with flowers on it. Once they were seated, Rose was excited about the other secret Arnie wanted to share.*

ROSE: I want to thank you for sharing about going for counseling. I know that was a big step for you.

ARNIE: You were right: It was not easy. It can be difficult to talk about feelings. But I like my counselor and think he is helping me a lot.

NARRATOR: *Arnie and Rose share a bottle of wine together. There is a lot of hand-holding going on. They both seem very happy.*

ROSE: I thought about asking you a lot of questions regarding counseling, but for now let's just enjoy being together.

ARNIE: Here's my other secret.

NARRATOR: *Arnie slowly moves from his chair and comes over to Rose. He gets down on one knee and takes out a box from his jacket. Rose starts to cry. Then Arnie opens the box.*

ARNIE: Will you do the honor, sweet Rose, of marrying me?

ROSE: Yes, yes, yes! You have just made me the happiest girl in the world!

ARNIE: No happier than me.

ROSE: I love you so much. This ring is so beautiful, and it fits perfectly. I cannot wait to spend the rest of my life with you.

ACT III

SCENE 1

NARRATOR: *Sheriff Beth, Betty Sue, and Dee are having lunch at the Do Good Diner in the neighboring town of Kingsford. Betty Sue asked her two friends to join her.*

<u>SHERIFF BETH</u>: I feel like the odd person out here. You both heard about the changes at Muffin World before I did. However, I have some news you two may not know about. One of my deputies was at Happy Times for dinner last night and saw Arnie propose to Rose.

<u>BETTY SUE</u>: Are you kidding? That is great news. I am so happy for them.

<u>DEE</u>: Me too. How exciting.

<u>BETTY SUE</u>: I asked you two here to gossip about changes at Muffin World. But now maybe we should think about planning a wedding shower for Rose.

<u>NARRATOR</u>: *The three friends spend the next hour sharing ideas and excitement about all of the good news.*

QUESTIONS/THOUGHTS

- Have you ever lived in or visited a small town?
- Where do you think Rose and Arnie should go on their honeymoon?
- Have you been to a wedding?
- What do you think will happen next in the play?

SCENE 2

<u>NARRATOR</u>: *I just heard from Rose that Arnie proposed to her. I am thrilled but also know they have had their ups and downs in the past. I am looking forward to helping them any way I can. I will need to work on being a good listener and not trying to take over. I am also thinking about what to give them for a wedding gift. I know Rose's mother, who died five years ago, would be very happy. I can hear her say, "Now, Rudy, do everything you can to make our little Rosie happy." My eyes are tearing, but I am full of joy. By the way, Rose is in her office at Muffin World with Rocco.*

ROSE: I am very proud of the changes you have made, Rocco. I had my doubts, but you proved me wrong. A lot of people have told me how well you are doing.

ROCCO: This is a wonderful compliment. Thank you, Rose.

ROSE: You deserve it. Because you have done so well, I would like you to be part of our team as we are making changes here. With that would come a full-time job making $2.00 more per hour. My idea is to make you an assistant baker, learning from Arnie and Uncle Rudy. What do you think?

ROCCO: I cannot believe it. Of course, I want to do this. Can I hug you?

ROSE: Of course you can. I am expecting big things from you, Rocco.

NARRATOR: *A big hug follows with tears and happiness from both Rose and Rocco.*

SCENE 3

NARRATOR: *Arnie has had his first snowboard lesson with Joanie, Lockhart, and Rocco. At the last minute, Betty Sue asked to join the group. There was plenty of snow, and everyone was eager to learn. With help from Arnie and Lockhart, Joanie was able to join in just fine. At the end of the lesson, Rocco started a snowball fight. A lot of laughs and joking went on for quite a while. Afterward, Arnie treated the group to hot chocolate and warm pretzels in the ski lodge.*

ARNIE: I hope you all had a blast today. Everyone tried hard. I think you will all be snowboarding like pros in no time. I also want to thank you for supporting Rose and me over the past few weeks. I know a lot of changes are taking place.

BETTY SUE: I think change can be a good thing. Sure, it takes some getting used to, but it can also be exciting. I stopped smoking ten years ago, and I am so glad I did. But boy, was it hard to make the change.

JOANIE: Starting a full-time job, dealing with being in a wheelchair, and advocating for myself will be a big challenge for me. I am excited and scared at the same time. However, I need to grow up. I am very happy that Rose thinks I can help grow the business using my social media skills.

LOCKHART: Good for you, Joanie. You go, girl! Your future is so bright. You have a great attitude.

JOANIE: Many thanks, Lockhart. Those words mean a lot coming from you. Having you as my job coach and friend has meant everything to me.

ACT IV

SCENE 1

NARRATOR: *Six months later. Before the wedding, Rose had her bachelorette party in Chicago. Arnie and his three high-school friends went skiing in Colorado for his party. Rose and Arnie had their wedding at the local ski lodge. Over one hundred people came.*

I made the wedding cake, and of course, it was beautiful. Betty Sue and her band rocked the night away. Right now, they are on a five-day honeymoon in New Orleans. Let's listen in.

ARNIE: This place has so many great restaurants and bakeries. I cannot believe it.

ROSE: My head is full of new ideas for our bakery back home in Iron Mountain.

ARNIE: I would love to start making French donuts, which they call *beignets*.

ROSE: We could try lots of things. First, I think we need to figure out what goodies might sell the best. Maybe we need to take a break from work and focus on enjoying our honeymoon.

ARNIE: How about we take a paddleboat trip on the Mississippi River. Later we can come back and listen to jazz at a local nightclub.

ROSE: Don't forget an amazing dinner and late-night walk on Bourbon Street.

ARNIE: I am so happy we finally got married.

ROSE: Me too! I could not be happier.

SCENE 2

NARRATOR: *After Arnie and Rose got back from their honeymoon, they were excited to redo the bakery. They even set a date for the grand opening. However, there were problems. The new oven had not yet arrived. The city was dragging its feet on approving the remodeling plans. The new sign for the bakery was delayed in Toledo, and guess what else? Betty*

Sue got a new full-time job as a singer and bartender in Nashville, Tennessee. She felt awful leaving her best friend but could not pass up a really good job. Now we find Rose with Dee, at Dee's house.

ROSE: Thanks for seeing me, Dee. I really need to talk to someone.

DEE: What is on your mind, Rose.

ROSE: I am at the end of my rope. There have been so many delays with the grand opening. Also, Betty Sue is leaving this week for her new job in Nashville. We have been best friends forever. I am not sure I can handle all the changes and roadblocks in my life right now.

DEE: How can I help?

ROSE: Maybe you can listen and give me advice.

DEE: Listening, I can do. As far as advice, here is what I have to say:

- It is hard to go through hard times alone, so don't.
- Don't be afraid to ask for help.

- Life is full of highs and lows.
- Take deep breaths.
- In hard times, try to look for something or somebody that will bring a smile to your face.
- Never stop believing in yourself.
- Try not to close yourself off from others around you.

I sure as heck don't have all the answers, Rose. You are a strong woman, and I am sure you will see through the hard times. I am here for you whenever you want to talk some more. Keep the faith, Rose!

ROSE: What you say makes great sense, Dee. I'm still feeling frustrated, though. I have to believe things will get better. I knew it would help to talk with you.

QUESTIONS/THOUGHTS

- Who do you talk with when you are having problems?
- Why do you think Rose chose Dee to share with?
- What advice would you have given Rose?

<u>NARRATOR</u>: *Rose thanks Dee for her time and advice. After getting into her Ford pickup truck, she starts talking to herself.*

<u>ROSE</u>: Listen here, sister, it is now or never. You must be strong. Continue to focus on your goal of building a successful business and enjoying life outside of work. Do not give up. Ask for help when you need it. You have a great new husband, so don't forget that. It is time to kick some butt. Make Rudy and mom proud.

SCENE 3

<u>NARRATOR</u>: *It took a few months before the bakery could open. Several more challenges came up. Rose, however, stayed strong, and the whole town got behind her. Thanks to Joanie, there was a lot of excitement about today's grand opening. She helped spread the word over social media. The crowd outside the bakery was huge.*

What Do You Want on Your Pancakes?

<u>ARNIE</u>: Hello, everyone. My name is Arnie. I am the head baker here at Rose and Rudy's Bakery Delights. This is a special day for us. Thank you for being here. To show our appreciation, all our donuts and muffins will be on sale half-price today. We also are giving free samples of our other bakery items. Before we open the doors, I want to introduce our staff and express deep appreciation for them and the more than fifty volunteers who helped set up the new store. Lastly, I have some good news and bad news. The bad news is that Rose cannot be with us today, because she is not feeling well. The good news is that she and I are expecting a baby. Rose was so disappointed she could not be here today. However, she asked me to read the following:

Muffin World

Dear family, friends, and neighbors,

Rose and Rudy's all the way
Welcome to our bakery today
Hope you enjoy our sweet delights
Take lots and lots of bites.

Tell one, tell them all
From big towns to small
We want everyone to know
We are ready to show.

Give a hoot and a holler
I said bring them by the collar
Once inside our tasty place
Will soon be a smile on their face.

What Do You Want on Your Pancakes?

Friends have seen us through
They have been true blue
Thanks for all you do,
You and you and you.

My love to everyone today
Thanks for coming our way
You make the world go round
I am glad we live in the same town.

So long and be happy! Love, Rose.

<u>NARRATOR</u>: *For those of you reading this play, I hope you enjoyed it. I am going to leave it to you on how the play should end. Here are a few things to think about.*

QUESTIONS/THOUGHTS

- Do you think Arnie and Rose will have a baby boy or girl?
- Do you have any names for the baby?
- Would you like to work at a bakery or just be a customer?
- Rose and Arnie got lots of support from our family, friends, and neighbors. Who do you get support from?
- If you were coming to Rose and Rudy's bakery, what would you like to taste first, second, third?
- Where is your favorite place to go in your town?

About the Authors

DR. ANKE GROSS-KUNKEL is a lecturer at the University of Cologne in the field of Pedagogy and Didactics for People with Intellectual Disabilities. Her work focus is on inclusive literacy and cooperation between special education and the subjects German and English. She also works in the field of participatory education and research with people with intellectual disabilities (within the inclusive summer school project SUSHI) and cancer patients with disabilities.

What Do You Want on Your Pancakes?

Besides doing research on literature participation by people with intellectual disabilities, Dr. Anke Gross-Kunkel has implemented over fifty Next Chapter Book Clubs in Germany and other European Countries in cooperation with the nonprofit organization KuBus®.

• • •

GAIL RITTER spent thirty-eight years as an educator in New Jersey. Most of that time was spent in an eighth-grade language arts classroom. During that time, she found herself wearing a number of different hats, including newspaper advisor, debate coach, yearbook advisor, and faculty chairperson of the district professional development committee. Gail's professional career provided her with an uncanny ability to think on her feet, to appreciate the diversity of her students and their multiple styles of learning, and to realize the importance of a sense of humor, especially about herself.

Now retired in the Wilmington area of North Carolina, Gail divides her time between being the adoption coordinator for Monty's Home, a local dog-rescue/prison-training program, and being a facilitator in the Brunswick Forest chapter of the Next Chapter Book Club. Her children, their spouses, and her four grandchildren call her the busiest retired person that they know.

• • •

From Columbus, Ohio, with a Sociology degree from the University of Hawaii, **DESIREA DOOLIN** has always gravitated toward helping, teaching, and learning about others. Desirea has experienced life-altering workplace opportunities like assistant-teaching middle-school ESL students, supporting collegiate students as a resident assistant, leading a summer camp for adolescents with disabilities, and directing a day program for adults with disabilities.

Desirea currently works for Chapters Ahead Inc., onboarding and assisting all book clubs in the United States, Canada, and Australia. Through these experiences, Desirea learned valuable lessons that have guided her as she continues assisting adults with meaningful daily living tasks and community engagement. After twelve years in the field, Desirea has enjoyed working alongside and supporting people of all backgrounds, disabilities, and mental-health diagnoses. Desirea finds the work done at the Next Chapter Book Club to be very fulfilling and thinks it is a pleasure to watch the members further their learning and social development.

• • •

DR. TOM FISH spent most of his professional career as a faculty member and administrator at the Ohio State University Nisonger Center for Excellence in Developmental Disabilities.

About the Authors

He is noted for his work in developing transition programs for youth with high-functioning autism and pioneering services for siblings of individuals with developmental disabilities. Dr. Fish founded the Next Chapter Book Club, a community-based literacy program with over three hundred clubs in six countries. He has authored four books and relishes the opportunity to advocate with and for people with disabilities and their families any chance he gets. He enjoys traveling and playing the ukulele. Dr. Fish is also wild about his three children, their wives and soon to be husband, his five grandchildren, and his soulmate, Lyna.

www.ingramcontent.com/pod-product-compliance
Lightning Source LLC
Chambersburg PA
CBHW070331260626
47160CB00003B/1009